About the Author

The author was born in the west country but was educated in Norfolk. He spent the first twelve years of his working life in the British merchant navy working as a ship's radio officer but left the service due to its rapid decline. After working on several 'foreign' flag vessels, he decided things were not so much fun as they use to be. So, after a brief stint at Portishead radio, he left the sea completely and started working for an office supply company as a field engineer until taking early retirement and relocating to a small village in central Brittany for a slower pace of life

The Beginning

Mike Foreman

—

The Beginning

Vanguard Press

VANGUARD PAPERBACK

© Copyright 2024
Mike Foreman

The right of Mike Foreman to be identified as author of
this work has been asserted by him in accordance with the
Copyright, Designs and Patents Act 1988.

A CIP catalogue record for this title is
available from the British Library.

ISBN 978 1 83794 212 1

This is a work of fiction. Names, characters, businesses, places, events and
incidents are either the product of the author's imagination or used in a
fictitious manner. Any resemblance to actual persons, living or dead, or actual
events is purely coincidental.

*Vanguard Press is an imprint of
Pegasus Elliot Mackenzie Publishers Ltd.*
www.pegasuspublishers.com

First Published in 2024

**Vanguard Press
Sheraton House Castle Park
Cambridge England**

Printed & Bound in Great Britain

Chapter One

My name is Olaf being born in the country of Norway in the year 881 of simple fisher folk, my father and his father before him having always been engaged upon this occupation. Although I was always avidly interested in the sea, as most men from the Northland's are, the one thing I knew already for sure was that I did not want to spend my life as my father and his father before him had, out on the fjord or near its distant entrance fishing day after day.

It was the only thing they knew how to do and the Fjord and the sea to the west of it being their entire world, it was their world but I did not intend to make it mine.

Although I had reached this decision at an early age in my life, it had taken me some time to summon the courage up to let my desires to be known to my father and grandfather. My grandfather was now at an advanced age and I knew that he in particularly would take my decision very hard, or so I had thought at the time, so I kept my feelings to myself for as long as I possibly could.

Often I would visit the port below the shale beach, with its rickety old quay, now so desperately in need of repair, where quite often a boat or two could be found moored there, not fishing vessels, but big ocean going vessels that I had heard traded with far away countries, over the north sea to countries called Scotland and Wessex and I had heard that often greater distances were undertaken, even to the land of the Franks, where many of our people had left our shores to go to this freshly found land, to settle there and never to return taking advantage of the free land, and the better climate, eventually marrying local women and as time passed no longer thinking of themselves as men of the northlands, this is what I wanted I told my father one day, to see these far away and strange countries, to sail upon those powerful sea going vessels that so often frequented our harbour. I thirsted for adventure it was so hard for me to put into words the way that felt so that he could perhaps understand me better. I think at times he thought that I just wanted to go raiding as so many of the other men of the adjacent villages did. It's dangerous and it's not right that you want to do something that will get you killed or at best you must realise that you will be ruining the lives of all the people that you come into contact with just to satisfy your need for wealth he told me on so many occasions. I tried in vain to say that that was not in my thoughts, that it was really the sight of foreign lands and the people who lived in these lands that intrigued me so much. He often just looked at me in that strange way that he had and shake his head saying we would talk of things later, which we never really did.

These conversations with him, if that's what they were, did nothing to dull my curiosity I even though at times that he had his own interests at heart and did not care about the things that I was beginning to hold so dear. So I would go down onto the dock most days, perhaps to spite and frustrate my father, I would pester the men working on these ships for information as to where they had been, what lands had they seen and was it true that the streets of Miklagard were paved with gold, and was it true the people living there had skins the colour of charcoal, who rode on beasts the colour of the sand and did these animals really have six legs and teeth as long as a seax. Also by the way, what country did the port of Miklagard lie in? I would like to go and see it one day soon. Often I received enthusiastic but much exaggerated answers to my questions, as is the way of sea faring men, other times for my pains it was just a cuff around the ear from the ships sailing master tired of me stopping his men from working.

I had often listened as a child to all the great saga's recited in the great long house, high above our harbour, often crawling under one of the tables, and chewing on a morsel of lamb that one of the men invariably passed down to me when they found me crouched in my supposed hiding place. Sometimes an old ship's captain when in his cups would start to relate stories from his youth, how he and others had sailed past the country of Iceland and seen the coast line of an unknown country, where high snow covered mountains reached to the sky and where the shorelines were inhabited by demons and the surrounding sea swarmed with fetches and sea serpents making a landing nigh impossible. How they knew that they must turn their ships around at the first favourable wind and return to Iceland less they get caught up in a maelstrom or such which would surely swallow their ship and the crew dragging them to the depths of the ocean where they would be forced to become mates to the sea witches and worse that lurked beneath the waves forever denied entry to the hall of Valhalla having died a useless straw death without sword or axe in hand.

As I grew older, my mind grew more set, none of this fishing for me I would often say to my friend, Bjorn, who was a number of years older than myself and a man who already had achieved a reputation as being a major asset to have amongst your crew, and who was well on the way to becoming a warrior of some repute. He had been involved in a couple of skirmishes against some renegade Danes the previous year, where all conceded that he acquitted himself well. It was him who encouraged me above all others of my friends to follow my heart's desire. Always the first to agree with me that fishing was not the way to spend one's life, not for men such as us he would often say, it's the open sea, drink and women and pillage that keeps a Northman feeling that he is still alive, a statement I was to hear him repeat so many times over the coming years. I liked Bjorn and looked to him I now realise in retrospect, as being someone I wanted to model myself on, he already had several tattoos upon his upper arms and the crowning glory there was a single solid silver arm ring, given to him the previous year by the local Jarl for his part in the exploit against the Danes, it was a tremendous honour to have such a gift bestowed upon one, especially at such a young age, and I could only gaze at his arm ring with envy.

Although I was now of an age where I could go and help my father out on the fjord with his fishing, he also expected me now and then to accompany him further down the coast in search of better fishing grounds, when my father mentioned these up and coming voyages I suspected that he was just trying to show me that he did go to other places to fish and not just within the confines of our fjord. That life as a fisherman was not as boring as I seemed to think it was, but it mattered not to me, if I could find some excuse and avoid accompanying him then I would do so, hoping my father would perhaps understand that I really was not much interested in this way of life.

One of the other things that gripped my imagination as I grew to manhood, as well as wanting to travel to distant lands, was the use of the bow as both a weapon and for hunting, I use to spent hours down on the area of spare land behind the long house with the other youths of the village where we were taught how to use the sword and axe. We had no choice in the matter, how could you call yourself a man of the north lands if you could not use axe and sword, to protect yourself, your comrades and your ship. How could you become a warrior and at the end of your short life enter the hall of Valhalla. A short, glorious life as a warrior was the path Odin had laid out for most of us to follow, so my friend Bjorn continually told me

'Look around you Olaf, how many old men do you see here in our village? '

We were all instructed in the use of the bow as well, as soon as I saw my first bow it was something I knew I would have a life time involvement with, knowing also without question that I would excel in its use and be one of the best archers in our village. Little did I realise at the time that I would eventually assume the role of teacher, instructing all the other village youths in its use. As I became older and became part of the group, practising every day with sword and shield, the axe being favoured by many of the group, as it was with me, until the day arrived when I felt I had eventually mastered their use, if one can ever say one has truly mastered these weapons. But it was always the days that we were allowed to practice with our bows that I really looked forward to, shooting at targets affixed to bales of hay, or the bottom of old barrels, laid upon their side.

Chapter Two

Eventually, I think probably at my grandfather's bidding, my father came to me one day and told me that if it was still my desire not to follow him into the fishing occupation, then so be it, he having already apparently discussed the situation with my grandfather, and they had come to the decision that it would be acceptable to the family for me to go to sea and work on one of the numerous cargo vessels that plied their trade up and down the coast of Norway and further afield. Indeed he continued, he had already found me a place on his friend Harald's vessel, which I had heard about already and I knew they traded up and down the Norwegian coast to various small ports, it was true he went on to warn me that Harald did not undertake major voyages, due to the relatively small boat he owned.

When I began my already foreseen arguments, that this was hardly what I wanted, that I thirsted for the view of foreign shores, my father in retrospect, quite rightly informed me that before any ships master would employ me on a large ocean going vessel I would have to know my trade, thereby spending a couple of years on Harald's vessel would teach me the necessary seamanship skills I would require, and it would be a good enough place to learn them as any. He ended the conversation by saying this was to be the way of things or not at all, and that Harald's ship lay down in the harbour and I should show myself onboard first thing in the morning. Thus the decision was made for me, I knew I would have to do as my father wished, or be forced to join him working on our own fishing boat. I knew that Harald would be reporting back to my father on my progress and any wrong doings, it was not quite what I had envisaged. At least now thou I would be away from the life within our hum drum village where nothing ever seemed to happen and away from our fjord that seemed at times just to taunt me beckoning me towards the open sea that lay beyond and all the adventures that ocean offered but were at present denied to me. It also now dawned on me that I had after all an ally in my grandfather who I now realised had interceded on my behalf and that it was he who had been instrumental in putting me on the path to achieving my ambitions.

As I grew from childhood and became a man I now came to understand that my grandfather knew me better than my father did. The very next day saw me walking the short distance from our house to the harbour, clutching a sheepskin bundle that contained a few clothes and a brand new seax which my father had bought me as a farewell gift, it was complete with leather scabbard lined with sheep's skin to stop the blade from rusting, it must have cost him a small fortune. The gift was well appreciated by me, even thou I was likely to be away but for a short while, it was still a good gesture I thought. With thoughts of home and how things now seemed to be turning in my favour I followed the rock lined meandering path down to where Harald's boat lay moored, which was already a hive of activity making preparations to sail.

As soon as Harald saw me boarding his boat via the solitary plank which served as a gangway he cried out a greeting

'So you have decided to join us after all'

My first impression of Harald was that of a large jovial and friendly man. As I landed on the deck he came over to me, with him was a lanky somewhat skinny lad called Knut, I had seen him a few times before, he was a little bit older than myself and related to Harald, his sister's son I think. Harald introduced us and informed me that Knut would literally be showing me the ropes and would tell me what the work on the boat was all about, and I was to stay with him and learn all I could. He would also show me to a place where I could stow my possessions and eat and sleep. Things seemed to be getting off to a good start I thought, especially as Knut turned out to be an amicable and easy-going youth and I thought not likely to cause me problems for no reason, as it turned out we quickly became good friends. This trip was going to be fairly short my new found friend Knut informed me, we were just going up the coast to a port that lay no more than two days sail away, so we would be back in our own village within a week, a bit more maybe, not bad for a first trip he said, at least I would have more of an idea when I returned if I was going to like the sea going life or not. So began my apprenticeship onboard the trading vessel Starling, which was to last just over two years, and was an enjoyable part of my early young life.

We voyaged mostly up and down the Norwegian coast, taking small cargos from one small port to another, I would not say that I was un-happy as to the way things had turned out, I was learning the business of seamanship from Harald and his nephew, and life was without doubt more enjoyable here on Harald's boat than what was previously supposed to be my lot of working on my father's fishing vessel where I would most likely have got more and more discontent, until it provoked a major argument between the two of us and perhaps causing a un resolvable rift between us forever, and ending with me leaving home without his blessing.

We were back in our home port, sometimes a couple of times a month, but hardly ever being away for more than five or six weeks at a time. When we docked at our home port, I always returned home to my father's house, Thou I was always a bit careful as to what I said when he, and my now decidedly aged grandfather, spoke about their fishing trips, I think in retrospect that I was a bit of a disappointment to the two of them, I knew my father would definitely have preferred me to have taken to fishing, and eventually taken the boat over from him, as he had from his own father. I think that my grandfather however was able to accept the situation and my decision more readily than my father, but at least in the end the two of them had respected my wishes and had let me more or less go my own way.

Chapter Three

One crisp morning in early autumn I was up well before dawn, the frost was laying heavy upon the ground, it looked as if it could snow later in the day as the sky was still clouding over. My grandfather already had a welcome fire in the grate, which was well ablaze, with a pot of oatmeal simmering away and almost cooked, my father I noticed was sitting quietly in the corner of the room on a stool already pre-occupied thinking about his day's fishing out on the fjord and was busy tying fish hooks onto a long line.

'You are of up to Bjorgvin today with some cattle and farming implements I hear, there should be a good profit in it I would think, well at least for Harald.'

My grandfather said with a wink.

'It will take no longer than a month, I will be back before you know I've even gone,' I replied

'I'm hoping to do well out of this trip, Harald's a fair man and tries to pay us well, if things go to plan he's promised us all a bonus so we will see what happens.'

So with those brief comments and an equally brief goodbye to the pair of them, I wrapped my cloak around myself and made my way down to the quay. The Starling was lying against the quay; she had been moved up the quay a few feet since I had last seen her, which was probably three days or more ago, she had most likely been moved to help aid the loading of our cargo of cattle. As I got closer I could already see that the deck cargo of farming implements had already been brought aboard.

We had planned to sail just before noon, I could see strait away Harald was not happy, his sailing master Eysteinn seemed equally perturbed, and it was obvious why, the sky by now had become heavily overcast and laden with rain or perhaps snow which had the pair of them continually looking upwards, and as I followed their gaze I could understand their consternation, we were in for a storm and it looked as if it could be a bad one. I could hear snatches of conversation between the two of them, Eysteinn was advocating caution due to the approaching storm, and saying that perhaps it would not be a good idea to get caught in a heavy storm and the accompanying swell as we battled our way out of the fjord and into the open ocean. Harald seemed to be having none of it, replying that they must sail immediately and not delay, to delay would mean missing the favourable currents along the coast and also having to keep the cattle onboard overnight, or even worse, if the port became storm bound they would have to off load the cattle, and all the time and expense that would incur was beyond thinking about, not to mention of course the response from the cargo owners who already had arranged a buyer for the cattle with some people up in Bjorgvin. Harald I knew desperately wanted things to go right on this trip, the farm implements could wait if need be, but he desperately needed to successfully deliver this cargo of cattle because it would mean repeat business, a thing Harald could not afford to miss out on, things were getting tough for Harald financially, although the boat continually had work it could be doing a lot better. Often we would be forced into the situation where we had to take smaller and smaller cargos to ports maybe a couple of days sail away which was most times hardly financially justified Harold only undertaking these voyages to keep the boat and his men in gain full employ. Harold knew that he had to take what work was available and knew too well the consequences of letting the boat and more importantly his men lay idle, without cargos he could not pay them and they would soon drift away and find other work.

Harald being the ship's owner, naturally had his way in the argument with Eysteinn, so shortly before noon two men on the quay dropped our bow and stern lines into the water and we pulled them in, coiling them as we went and stowed them in their locker. Harald liked his boat tidy and well manned. I looked up at the sky and then across to Eysteinn, he caught my glance and just shook his head, he was worried which was unusual for him but there was nothing more to do other than just get on with it and hope things went well, all things at times were a calculated risk, one never really knew when the weather would turn foul on you.

It was Harald's boat after all and we knew that he would not take un-acceptable risks with it. If the storm broke while we were still in the fjord, there were numerous places to take shelter. If we made it out to sea and got ourselves well away from the coast it would be rough, especially with cattle onboard, but the boat was built for this purpose and these waters, so all should be well I told myself. Knut came across and joined me on our oar bench, for once he was quiet and from that I knew he was as scared as me. We rowed out into the middle of the fjord and raised our sail, the wind took it immediately and we began to pick up speed the sky above us was black as pitch, but the wind was surprisingly moderate.

I heard Knut muttering to the man on the oar bench in front of him that perhaps all would be well,

'Aye lad,' came the reply.

'But we will all get a good soaking for sure and have to stay that way until we make port.'

These boats were always wet, your clothes and equipment sometimes turning green with mould, it was just a fact of life onboard, something else to endure but nobody really got used to it and I had already found out in life that there was very little point in complaining about things especially if it's beyond one's power to do anything about it, just except it and move on was all you could expect to do

A couple of hours later and we were in a heavy swell, the cattle not liking it one little bit more than we did, then worse a fork of lightning streaked across the sky, followed immediately by a clap of thunder as if Thor himself had just farted after a heavy meal. The very heavens seemed to open, never in my life had I seen such rain it was so heavy it flattened the sea and the lookout in the prow called out that he could see next to nothing in front of the boat. The sail had been reefed some time earlier and thus we continued for some hours, the light was failing quickly and now it would be impossible we all realised to be able to keep our bearings, we were a couple of leagues of shore, but there were numerous rocks to seaward of us, some almost warranting being called islands, but worse still there was numerous half submerged rocks out there, not normally a problem in good visibility but now they weighted heavily in our thoughts.

We survived the night, the dawn not only bringing light but an abatement in the storm that had raged all night. We hoisted our sail, the better to control the vessel and to try to get back on course. Harald and his nephew moved forward to join the lookouts in the prow, trying to see something recognisable and thus get our bearings, the lookouts having up to now indicated nothing amiss, apart from the obvious poor visibility. I was hanging onto the mast trying to keep my feet, the cattle were making a fearful noise, as if they were aware of some approaching catastrophe, and the stench from them was fearsome, there is nothing worse than a cargo of thirsty untended seasick cattle.

The rain had stopped and the visibility lifted considerable and then suddenly there was a cry of alarm from the lookouts in the prow of the ship

'Breakers directly ahead,' they were yelling.

I could see them myself now, it was almost like it was a dream; this impending disaster about to unfold was going to happen to somebody else and their ship but not to us. Here before us lay a rocky coastline, whether large island or the mainland itself we had no way of knowing, not that it mattered anyway, within minutes we had struck. As we had tried to sheer away, the vessel ploughed right up onto jagged rocks, with the starboard side of the vessel being literally ripped away; the force of our grounding driving our cargo of heavy farm implements strait through what remained of the vessel's side, quickly followed by cattle, men and everything else.

I felt myself plucked away; my hold on the mast broken and felt myself being propelled through the air like a child's rag doll, and I remembered nothing else until, what I assumed was some hours later. Eysteinn was standing over me gently shaking me by the shoulder, I found myself propped up with my back against a rock, Eysteinn and another man were looking down at me, I noticed another man lying on the sand just a few feet away from me, he looked to still be alive but injured by the look of him. Every bone in my body hurt, I was freezing cold and felt numb to my bones, but all my limbs seem to work. The storm by now had totally blown itself out, the surf was high and I could see wreckage and worse still there were already bloated bodies of men and cattle being tossed this way and that in the surf, some lying above the tide line. Where is everyone else, is this all that has survived I asked of Eysteinn.

'I think so,' he replied. 'There may be one or two more that survived and that we will come across shortly, but I doubt it'

Anticipating my next question he said

'No lad, Harald and Knut have both perished, they were up in the prow of the ship with the other two lookouts, they had no chance of surviving, they have gone with all the others to Odin's hall'

Two days and nights we were on the beach of what turned out to be an island, we almost froze to death, but were luckily spotted by a couple of small fishing boats who came right through the surf and almost up onto the beach and took us of that God's forsaken island and back to their village. Two days or so later when we had regained our strength sufficiently to leave, we made our way back home to tell our sad story there.

Chapter Four

When I returned home after the Starling had wrecked on that miserable island my father once more set about asking me of my plans for the future, had I perhaps had time to think on things and maybe reconsidered my decision about working on his boat fishing out in the local fjord with him. There were a lot of benefits he said that I was not considering, the chance of being home most evenings, the opportunity to marry a local girl and to raise a family it was a good village that we lived in plenty of people to buy our catch of fish. He was I know building up to say that I could be given a greater say in the running of the business and start to think about taking over the boat completely in the near future. I think thou that he already knew what my reply would be without his need for asking, and my stubborn appearance that first evening back at home made him not want to waste his breath on me and persist with his request with any vigour. He eventually ended up my saying if that's the way you want it Olaf, If you still want to voyage to distant lands, then so be it and I will not stand in your way any more. I suggest then that you go down to the dock in a couple of days' time, there will be a large ocean-going vessel docking soon, I would hazard a guess and say that she will be in port for a week or more. They will need to re provision before they sail again and I think the ship's captain is looking for a couple of new crew members which rumour has it, he would ideally like to come from our village here, men who now the coast and it's ports hereabouts. But where they are really going once they leave the safety of our fjord I have no idea, maybe it's local work but no one seems to be privy to such information especially where this ship's captain is concerned

My father informed me that he slightly knew the ship's captain from a few years back, a man called Arn who had started to use the dock in our fjord again on a regular basis, he had now obtained a larger vessel, and the dock he had previously been using near the entrance to our fjord, was now proving to be inadequate and not sheltered enough for his new vessel. The access down there for the horse drawn carts to load and unload the cargo was he felt also poor for the larger wagons now needed. My father went on to say that he had broached the subject with Arn suggesting that now he had a larger vessel, it was likely be he would need an extra man or two to help him crew his vessel in the near future, so I have asked him to consider taking you on Olaf. I have spoken with him at length and told him of the two years you spent on the Starling sailing with Harald and the sort of voyages that you have been engaged in, so that I could give him an idea about the kind of seafaring experience you have gained. I think that the conversation went well; Arn said that he had known Harald for several years, and also knew he was not one to tolerate slackers on his vessel, so he told me that he thought you must have learned your trade well under Harald's guidance. I have also mentioned that you are a promising bowman and already have considerable skill with axe and shield, which went down well with the man I think.

There it was again, my father trying to dictate the path my life was to follow, but I guessed all fathers to be the same and all would try and put their sons on what they saw to be a good and safe path. This time I could offer no argument, I had already heard people speaking of Arn and his vessel and already knew that he undertook major voyages, to faraway places not just across the north sea and around the coast to Wessex, but also to the Shetlands and the Orkneys and I had even heard it rumoured he went up to Iceland, to where it was rumoured the world ended just beyond the western horizon, the sea turning into a boiling maelstrom where fetches and sea serpents lived and would reach up from the depths and pluck you from your ship and drag you to the ocean's bottom to a watery grave, and thus deny you any chance of entering Odin's hall.

I went down to the dock immediately the next morning, even thou my father had told me the vessel would not dock for several days, but I didn't want anyone else to snatch away what I already considered to be my place upon Arn's boat. Of course the quay was empty save a couple of small fishing skiff's unloading their nights catch. The next two mornings were a repeat of the first, but on the fourth morning I went back down to the dock once more and as soon as I rounded the bend in the road I could see a flurry of activity centred around a massive vessel, a dragon heads prow painted red, with green eyes, which seemed to bore into me as if to question who it was who had the audacity to thus approach, it's red sail neatly furled, oars stowed away and ropes coiled, giving the overall impression of a well-run ship and disciplined crew. Thus I caught my first glimpse of the magnificent seagoing vessel "Sea eagle" thou I didn't know it at the time she was destined to be my home for many years to come. I came up to the vessel which was securely tied up with strong ropes both forward and aft, gently nudging the quay now and then with the movement of the current, a solitary boarding plank from shore to the centre of the vessel affording the only way onboard, I waited my turn behind a couple of other men who were about to board the vessel and when the plank was clear of people coming down onto the dock I followed these two men up and was about to step onto the vessel only to find my path was blocked by a large burly heavily bearded man, who asked me what my business onboard his ship was.

I quickly replying that my name was Olaf and that I had come to see the ship's captain about employment.

' Well boy my name is Ivar, and I am this ships sailing master, I suppose that you are Svein's boy, he was onboard the ship last time we were in port here, and spoke to us of you, we heard of the loss of Harald and his boat, what a tragedy, a good ship and captain both gone before their time. We had half expected you not to show up, anyway the captain's busy right now so find yourself somewhere out of the way and I will return with Arn when he's concluded his business.'

I found myself a seat on one of the rowing benches, these benches also doubled as a locker for stowing personnel items, such as clothes and weapons; I hoped the owner would not mind me using his bench, as I thought that maybe I could well be in for a bit of a wait. After what seemed an eternity of sitting there, just watching the unloading of the vessel, most of which was familiar activity to me by now after two years of working on Harald's vessel. A man came up to me with a smile upon his face and greeted me, saying his name was Tor, I had noticed that he had been watching me for a few minutes and now he came and sat on the bench beside me, offering me some bread and cheese and a gulp or two from his ale flask, we were later joined my another man who Tor introduced to me as Reidar, both spoke Norse with an accent and were obviously not local men, perhaps from the far southwest of the country I thought, but both were friendly enough towards me and they seemed already to know my purpose for being onboard, saying that it was a foregone conclusion that Arn and Ivar would give me a place onboard the ship, but don't say anything stupid warned Reidar, and it's worthwhile remembering that Arn doesn't like to hear his men moaning or complaining of things, bear that in mind for our future voyages, it will hold you in good stead with him. Reidar then going on to say that the vessel was indeed shorthanded as I most likely already knew and that Arn had already taken on another new man called Bjorn from this very village here, and did I know him?

Well, Bjorn's kept that pretty close to his chest I thought, but with that news it increased my resolve to make a good impression with the ship's captain, to sail on this vessel with such men as Bjorn and my two new friends who sat here beside me would be more than I could have ever dreamed of. Eventually I spotted Ivar coming across to me, Tor and Reidar by now having returned to their duties, with him was a stocky man, walking across the deck with that unmistakable seaman's roll, his face creased by years of exposure to sun and wind at sea, deep lines etched into his skin as if they had been carved there, and a face that one immediately knew was used to smiling, eyes that almost squinted at you and that missed nothing. His whole countenance left you in no doubt that you were in the presence of a man who had immense strength of character. He just stood there and looked me over and eventually giving that smile I was to see so often, saying as he turned to Ivar

'He will do'

And that was my first introduction to Arn whom I was to get to know extremely well and to be able to count as friend, to be able to call such a man friend was in itself a privilege and a friendship that was to last the rest of our lives. Ivar passed a few words with Arn before he went back to his business in organising the loading of the new cargo being taken on here. Ivar turned back to me and told me that the vessel was due to sail for Iceland in a few days' time, dismissing me with a wave of his hand he told me to go back home and say my goodbyes to my father, and that I was to return here at first light the day after tomorrow with all my kit. By the way I have heard that you are a good bowman, so make sure you bring your bow, also your axe and shield and a helmet if you have one. We may be a peaceful trading vessel Olaf, but we are continually harassed by those accursed Danes outcasts and will be in danger from them until we are a couple of days away from the coast and on our way to our destination in Iceland, so we need to be able to defend ourselves should they be stupid enough to try and board us on the open sea.

As I departed down the boarding plank, I was given a cheery greeting by a man who I recognised immediately as one who often came to our house, and was friend to my father, his name was Hans, he was a bit of an odd bird who lived just outside the village in a large house at the base of the mountain with his wife, their only son having been killed just recently I heard, in a fight out at sea when his boat was attacked by marauders. I think Han's repaired sea boots and the like for the village when he was not at sea.

'I hear we are to be shipmates he called out, don't be late on sailing day'.

The next day or so seemed an eternity, I could hardly wait to be away and join my new comrades onboard Arn's ship, I nailed a new leather strip around the edge of my shield, I polished my hardened boiled leather helm so much, that my grandfather eventually warned me it would likely fall to pieces, I sharpened my axe blade so that you could have almost shaved with it and sat by the roaring fire fidgeting with this and that, even our old dog sensed a change in me and kept out of my way. I tried hard not to show my impatience with my old grandfather, as he tried to engage me in trivial conversation, trying to get me to tell him what my long term plans might be, but he was to receive few sensible answers from me, however as usual he was tolerate of me and I think perhaps understood me more than I gave him credit for, just as my father was the opposite of him and still did not comprehend why I had to go and maybe risk my life on deep sea voyages even thou it was him who had in reality had secured the berth on Arn's boat.

'In Odin's name boy what are you looking for '

He cried out on the last morning that I was to see him for a while, as he boarded his small skiff and hoisted its sail to go out to the fishing grounds the other side of our fjord.

'Olaf I hope this voyage gets the madness out of your system and when you return home you will have come to your senses and will be ready to come and join me in fishing on the fjord, it's what all of our family has ever done, it's a good living and has provided for us well'

The rest of what he said was lost to me as the wind took his sail and he rapidly tacked out into the fjord. The hell with him I muttered under my breath as I trudged back home, briefly saying my farewells to my grandfather, who handed me a sheepskin roll which contained the few personnel possessions which I intended taking with me.

'This will come in handy.'

He said as he passed me a large brand-new whet stone. I took his arm, looking into his grey, watery eyes and said

'Thank you for making this all possible grandfather.'

With those few final comments I slung my shield upon my back also hanging my helm by its leather strap from my belt, I made sure my seax was there in my belt, shouldered my axe and started to make my way down the path that led to the quay and towards Arn's boat and to unknown adventures and to see what kind of fate had been planned for me, good or bad it was all in the hands of Odin now. A few hundred yards or so down the path and I heard a shout from behind me, turning I immediately recognised a man called Gurt, who was puffing and panting as he caught up to me, asking me to wait for him. Gurt owned a small farm up in the hills which he ran with his wife and two sons, both boys being my age or perhaps a year or so older, I think he was on hard times and had returned to seafaring to make some extra money, he was my father's age and I think he now considered his 'sons were capable of keeping the farm together while he was absent. Tor had mentioned the other day to me that the man would be joining us for this trip, and indeed it would not be the first time he had sailed with Arn, despite his age he was still a true man of the north and still looking for adventure, I had spoken to him on many occasions and he was a man very easy to warm towards. Things were looking good I thought as I walked in amicable silence with Gurt the final short distance down towards the quay, my friend Bjorn now part of our crew and now Hans and Gurt, at least I won't feel like a complete outsider.

Gurt and I arrived at the dock a few minutes later, our arrival being noted by Ivar who waved us onboard and gave Gurt a warm welcome, with just a nod of recognition in my direct, I didn't expect more, after all Ivar knew nothing about me other that I had served on Harald's boat, and that had hardly ended well. Arn had taken me onto his vessel as an extra hand, and maybe he was thinking it was just out of respect for my father that I was being given a chance to prove myself on Arn's boat, had it been left to Ivar maybe it would have been a different story, who knows, but as time went on I found that I had no cause for complaint about the man, and he always treated me fairly.

Then with a flourish of his hand Ivar indicated the group of men already stowing their gear in their lockers which also served as their row benches.

'Gurt you can pick your own row bench and oar companion'

Turning to me he said

'Olaf I want you to pair up with Ulf, he's a good rower with a strong arm he's been onboard a while, so knows the boat well, so listen to him carefully. He can teach you a lot, and he's a damn good man to have around in a fight. His one down fall is he likes his mead, so if he's drunk it's best to keep out of the bastard's way as he will fight anyone just because they are there standing in front of him, and he won't remember a damn thing about it in the morning when he's sobered up. So be warned!

Two hours later we slipped our mooring lines and rowed out into the fjord, I thought I could see my father's fishing skiff in the distance, so with one backward glance at the skiff and another at the dock where I could just about see our house, and where I knew my old grandfather would be standing up on the hill behind the house watching as we set sail.

I was glad to see Iceland, the voyage had been without incident and not to arduous, but I was cold and damp, and most of the time it had been just cold food that we were given. It was also my first really long voyage and it's surprising how the cold, the lack of hot food and the constant motion of the boats wears one down, the starling had been different, we were seldom out at sea for more than three or four days. Some of the men onboard were twice my age, but seemed not to show any sign of fatigue, but I know that they were just as glad to see the island looming up out of the mist as much as I was. We had a lot of cargo, farming implements, pots and pan, bolts of cloth and all the other commodities that the people here had need of.

After we had docked we began getting the boat sorted out, putting the oars into their trees and reefing the sail and safely stowing all ropes and such like away, all had their own lockers and special places to be stored. Arn I had noticed had been looking at the pair of us and came across and spoke to Ulf. It was still quite early and the shore side gang had only just started discharging the cargo, it was good just to watch for once and to see someone else sweating instead of us. There was not much we could do to help anyway, as local men were employed for the task and they wouldn't take kindly to us taking their work away from them. So we took advantage of the situation and just sat there on our row benches, just kicking our heel which is probably what had attracted Arn's attention towards us.

'Ulf the boys done well and I know you have not had much shore time of late, I want the pair of you to run an errand for me and then take a couple of days away from the ship'

'You know where old Magnusson's lives? go up there with Olaf and ask Magnusson to come down to the dock, himself mine, not that halfwit of a son of his, there's some things I need to discuss with him and tell him to bring those charts with him that he promised me last trip, that's if he's finished them. After that go and get the boy a good meal and a couple of drinks, and find him a warm bed in one of the tavern's along the water front. I don't need the two of you for a couple of days. He threw Ulf a couple of coins and added, by Odin's oath thou I want the two of you capable of working when you return, and don't make me come looking for the pair of you, stay out of trouble'

Ulf had that expression of deep hurt of his upon his face, as I was to see so often, as much to say

'What me, cause trouble?'

He was about to follow this up and utter some other indignant remark, but quite rightly I thought, changed his mind at the last minute and just said

'Well, we will be on our way then'

He looked at me and nodded towards the gangway, and we both headed off in that direction without a backward glance and were over the side of the boat and onto the dock as quick as our feet would carry us.

'Two days without having to work Olaf my boy, the luck of Loki himself '

Ulf had been on the south west coast of Iceland many times before, and hinted that he had once lived here on a farm inland, but didn't elaborate on the statement. I rapidly came to the conclusion that there was not that much to see or do here anyway. Ulf took me through the docks and into what passed for the town. We entered a tavern where Ulf was immediately recognised by the bar keep, who was decidedly on the old side and a women who I took to be his wife, both were standing behind a trestle table that held all manner of drinking vessels, bottles and flasks and the like to be found in such places

It was not the sort of tavern I would have thought Ulf would have normally frequented, it was clean and the clientele seemed respectable, so what were we doing here; maybe I had miss judged the man. I must admit that I was only really interested in some food and a dry bed, and said as much to the old girl behind the serving counter, she fussed and clucked over me like an old hen, with Ulf and the woman's husband finding it amusing. She sat me at a table and a serving girl brought out a huge bowl of steaming mutton stew, with goblets of fat floating on the top, with all manner of other things in it. I remember it as being amongst one of the best meals I ever having eaten, all washed down with several pots of foaming ale. After finishing the meal the old women realised I was about to fall asleep where I sat, so she ushered me into a store room out the back, where there was a bed covered with a heavy sheep skin covering, I was asleep I think before my head even touched what passed for a pillow.

Ulf seemed to have disappeared completely, and no one knew where, or so they said. So I spent my time mainly in the warmth of the tavern, drinking ale, bedding the serving wench and speaking to whoever entered the place. When not in engaged in these occupations I just wandering around the town, if town it could be called. It took a while but suddenly it occurred to me why Ulf had brought me to this tavern, he basically had other business to conduct, as well as going to see Magnuson, he probably just didn't want me under his feet, not that I minded, his business was of no concern to me, and I think from what he had said about the farm, that he really had come from these parts originally, so he could be up to anything, so it was probably for the best I was in this tavern with its friendly people. I expect he thought he was doing me a favour finding me such a comfortable berth. A couple of days later, I was wondering if I should make my way back to the ship on my own, when Ulf entered the tavern, sober and clutching a bundle of what looked like clothes and a mead skin.

'Time we were away back to the ship Olaf,' he said.

And with no other explanation he walked back out again, after having given the old girl behind the bar a couple of coins, I thanked the old crone for her kindness towards me and followed Ulf out into the street.

Chapter Five

We returned to the ship to find the dockside a hive of activity, all of the cargo seemingly having been discharged by now and a great many crates and barrels in the process of being brought onboard and in the process of being stowed, presumably it was a return cargo, or maybe just some everyday supplies. I noticed a side of beef and a couple of live pigs being brought on board, the pigs squealing adding to the general melee, well at least it looked to me we would eat well on the return voyage. We returned directly to our home port, with Arn pushing both the boat and us hard, he wanted us to get back home as soon as the god's would allow, I think he was a bit disgruntled there was not a great deal of return cargo, Arn as always was looking to make a profit from any voyage, but in this instance it was obvious our return journey was not going to show much of a profit if anything at all.

I settled into the work on Arn's boat and slowly became accepted by the rest of the crew, it being made easier by the fact that I had some good friends on board, notably Bjorn and Gurt. Old Hans, although gruff and bad tempered by nature, was always willing to spent some time with me and teach me about knots and ropes, and now and then when the necessity arose he showed me how to repair a ripped sail and how to stitch a new eye in the sail to take a rope and the like.

When we went ashore and if ever I got into real trouble, which was more than likely as I seemed to have a knack of upsetting strangers when I had the drink upon me, usually it was some drunken tavern brawl that I had invoked, having upset the biggest of the locals and the outcome obvious to all except me, I would invariable pick myself up of the floor and look around to find my oar mate Ulf standing by my side, he never questioned whether it was I who had started the brawl or not, he most likely knew the answer to that question already. Of course as soon as my friend Bjorn realised what was happening he would involve himself as well, both looked no further than the fact I was an oar mate and a good brawl was after all a good brawl and no one afterwards ever remembered what it was about anyway.

We did many voyages up and down the Norwegian coast going to most of the small coastal ports from time to time, we would even cross the North Sea and occasionally sail down to the east coast of Wessex. Less often we picked up a voyage or two to the isles of Shetland or the Orkney and then perhaps over to Iceland. We now and then encountered Dane raiders out at sea, especially along the coast of Wessex and Scotland which was one of their favourite hunting grounds, but few dare give chase, we were a large vessel and invariable had our shields hung out in their rack along the top strakes of the boat, so they knew we were not just ordinary sailor men who were not

41

competent to take care of themselves in a fight, but that we were warriors as well, and would most likely stand and fight, when they did chance their luck and give chase and on the rare occasion they managed to overhaul us and to come along side of our boat, they usually took another closer look at us and decided there and then that we were probably not worth getting themselves killed over. A couple of times when they did manage to come along side of us and attempted to board us they invariably failed, Arn would position me with my bow in what he thought was the best vantage position for any forth coming affray, and as soon as the Danes saw me drop one or two of their crew mates it was usually enough. Any of them that made it to our decks would then have to face Ulf or Bjorn and the rest of our crew, so usually it was only half-hearted attacks from them, and slowly our boat began to gain a reputation amongst the Danes that we were one boat best left alone. As time went by and my experience of this life grew, the more I came to love it, I knew I would never want to do anything else, and I realised I had made the right choice in following my own heart and listening to my friend Bjorn's advice, to follow this path and embrace this way of life, all of which now seemed like an awfully long time ago.

My father was still alive and occasionally went out onto the fjord to fish, but most of the time he left it to his hired man to do the fishing. I always went home when in dock if Arn allowed me a few days away from work. I think in looking back that in those later years I enjoyed the time that I spent at my father's house when I was docked in port, my father long since having given up any notion of trying to persuade me into coming back to work on the family boat and to work the fjord for fish. He could see also that I had become relatively wealthy from my work upon Arn's boat, that I was happy with the life I had chosen for myself, so that was good enough for him.

We were about to set sail once again when Ulf surprised most of us the night before we left again for the isles of Shetland and Iceland by telling us all that once we arrived in Iceland he would be leaving the boat for good. The reason he gave being that he was going to go ashore and run his family's farm. Most of the crew and certainly myself now knew he was from Iceland, but nobody really knew much about him let alone the fact that he still had family in Iceland as well as the farm I had never asked him about where he had gone that first time we were ashore in Iceland, it was after all none of my concern.. Arn was taken by surprise as much as anyone, and tried to dissuade him, and asked him to stay a bit longer working on the boat, at least for another trip to think things over, but Ulf said his mind was set, that he had thought it over and there nothing else to say on the matter. He duly left the first day we docked in Iceland. I was perhaps not as surprised as some, he had been my oar mate for a long time now and we had shared that same row bench for months and spent hours talking about this and that. I also caste my mind back to the first time I was in Iceland and he had left me in that friendly tavern and promptly disappeared for a couple of days. Now it was clear to me where he had gone, I would miss my friend greatly as everyone else would onboard. He would be a difficult man to replace and that was no mistake.

On our return home and after several weeks of in activity I thought things were about to take a turn for the worse when Arn called all the crew together one evening in the local longhouse, we had been in port for a few weeks now both the boat and its crew still idle. Most of us had not been over concerned, but now there was something a foot, we could see Arn was getting the boat repaired and sooner or later we would be putting to sea again but till then we still had money in our pockets and were intent on making the most of it. Most of the men had returned to their families, others including myself were squandering our hard earn money on drink and whores. Now thou some men were beginning to drift away to look for work on other boats, as they were getting tired of being at home, consistently being nagged by their wives and now they yearned for the peace and solitude of the open ocean.

I duly arrived at the meeting house, which doubled as a tavern to find most of the crew already assembled there, plus about another twenty-five or so other men, some were local men that I already knew, others I vaguely recognised from previous years as having served on other local ships, some of them I had even sailed with in years gone by. A man called Bjarni was sitting with Arn at the top of the room, drinking their ale together and deep in conversation. Presently Arn rose to his feet and thanked us all for coming and said he had some good news for us, that we would be putting to sea shortly, but not immediately for Iceland as we had all supposed would be the case. He said that we now had some urgent business across the North Sea, in Scotland to be precise. There was something that we needed to attend to before we could do anything else. He nodded his head towards Bjarni and said

'We are going across the North sea with my friend Bjarni here and his crew at the request of some of our people living on the Scottish coast who have been having problems with their neighbours, apparently they don't have enough warriors over there to solve the situation themselves, and things have now taken a turn for the worse if that's at all possible, it's become obvious things have become out of control and it's far too late now for things to be rectified by diplomacy alone.

The white Christ priests are at the bottom of the problem, as well as trying to convert our people away from their true religion they are encouraging them to follow the religion of their nailed god, what they teach is abominable but worse still they are inciting the rest of the population to attack our fellow north men and their families and force them from their farms and land. It's so obviously a ploy on their behalf to be able to possess their farms and lands, the elders have seen it coming for a number of years. It's come to a head now and is quite unacceptable to our peoples leaders over there and they feel the time has come to act and that it might be best if the situation is resolved by outsiders.

Now listen up, we don't want the entire coast provoked into turning on our people and making matters even more untenable than they already are, so what we will do will seem to the local Scottish lairds as being just another raid by a couple of renegade long ships. The blame will undoubtedly fall upon the Danes or perhaps even Frisian raiders, so no problem there he said with a laugh. More to the point lads he continued, there's going to be money in it from this raid to finance my next voyage to Iceland, and money in each and every one of your pockets to do with as you will. Things are looking up, I know we don't normally go raiding, there's as much money to be made from honest trading usually, but times are harder now and we owe it to our people in Scotland to help them with their problem. I doubt if it's going to be any more dangerous than our trading voyages, but which of you has ever worried about that? The one thing is sure thou it's going to be a bit more exciting than the usual humdrum voyages over the north sea we undertake. It might even get some of that fat of you Gurt'

To emphasis his point he playfully poked old Gurt in the belly with his fore finger.

Old Borg chirped up saying

'Aye and maybe get some of us killed as well into the bargain I'm thinking '

'Well you can stay at home and look after your ducks and geese '

was Bjarni's quick reply, which provoked a fit of laughter amongst the men, Borg was getting on in years now and had been with Arn for as long as anyone could remember, and the thought of him staying at home when there was a good fight looming and more to the point the likelihood of much hack silver to be taken was completely implausible.

A few days later Bjarni and Arn's plans were put to motion as we boarded our long ships and headed out from our home Fjord out into the north sea and set sail due west for the east coast of Scotland. The voyage across the North sea was uneventful, the winds were favourable, the sea slightly choppy which had the wind taking the top of the waves and blowing it back as spray into our faces, all under a bright blue sky, it was exhilarating and made one feel that one was alive, a man of the northlands and indestructible and on a mission of revenge ordained by Odin himself. Our seamen or perhaps for this voyage better referred to as warriors took care of their weapons in their free time, those with mail coats were cleaning them with sand and vinegar until they gleamed in the early morning sunlight, and then after oiling them they stowed them in sacking or wrapped them in a sheep skin until the time that they would be needed in just a few days' time. The conversation onboard ship was at first I thought a bit disconcerting, it was just the talk of men out at sea, we could have been just going on a peaceful trading voyage, not one of violence and perhaps one where death and injury awaited some. We all knew that if news of our raid had preceded us there was more than a possibility that we could arrive to find a small army waiting for us as we beached our ships and started to wade ashore through the surf.

When we arrived on the coast we decided to beach our ships up the coast a mile or so away from the village and the monastery that we sought, we decided that we leave just a few of the men to guard our ships. Then the bulk of us would make our way towards the village on foot. If the villagers were foolish enough to still be in the village when we arrived we would kill all that stood in our way and hopefully be able to subdue the people who remained putting the very fear of Odin himself into them. It was then our intention to make our way towards the White Christ's holy place and deal with these arrogant self-opinionated men, who claimed to preach a new religion, a tolerant one, an enlighten one as they put it, but who were ultimately to blame for inciting the local people who lived in the nearby villages to turn on our people and into provoking them to rob and kill our brethren whom we knew to be just peaceful farmers and traders. Our people had been here for many years; they had come here as farmers and settlers, welcomed by the local people, some of them still traded with their knaars back across the North Sea, but mainly now up to the Orkney and Shetlands, they now considered themselves in the first instance to be men of these lands now, most of them had few connections back home, if indeed any at all. They had inflicted no harm on the local people who were here before them, indeed they had been living side by side with them for many years quite peacefully, some of the men marrying local women, until the uninvited arrival of the white Christ priests who came and built their monastery, and everything had changed for the worse.

We left our ships and made our way inland and then turned towards the village, where we had thought to catch the inhabitants totally unawares, but as soon as they realised that they were under attack they soon rallied themselves which left some of us with the impression that maybe this was not the first time that they had been attacked by axe welding men coming the sea. As we entered the outskirts of the village half a dozen horsemen thundering down upon us, they must have had a lookout on the coast who had reported our presence for them to have been able to respond so quickly. We had not quite unexpected them to have mounted warriors stationed here, let alone to even have a detachment of soldiers within the confines of the village to guard it. However it was not a problem, there were almost fifty of us and we were all heavily armed. These men didn't lack courage, but they were too few, and our archers brought them down before they could inflict any harm upon us. As we entered the centre of the village we at first met some stiff resistance, a dozen or so men, most likely being just ordinary villagers, who were armed with axe and shield rounded the corner of a longhouse and ran headlong into us, engaging us in some vicious fighting, more of them poured out of another longhouse, but without their mail shirts and helms, probably having just woken and just pausing long enough to pick up their swords and shields once they had realised what was a foot outside. If they had been better prepared and had a bit more advanced warning they could have been a more serious problem than they actually were, but as it was we pushed through them. We fired the thatch on their houses and barns, killing their pigs and chickens as we made our way through the village. We had been told to leave the women and children alone, it was not meant to be a massacre of innocents, just a harsh lesson to let them know that we could be back anytime we wanted, we really just wanted to put the fear of Odin into them and hopefully to bring them to their senses and make them leave our people alone in peace. The white Christ priests were our real objective.

We left the village in flames behind us and made our way the short distance up to the monastery, and once there we were able to force our way into their so-called holy place with ease, a few of the white Christ priests offered us a token resistance but we cut them down where they stood without mercy. Bjarni's men once unleashed upon the white Christ monks were like a pack of wild dogs. It sickened me to see how they behaved but it was pointless to try and intervene. Bjarni was hardened to this kind of thing and would not condemn it. I had been involved in skirmishes out at sea and fought men who had tried to board my vessel but this was my first blood raid and I had no idea that a raid was going to be like this

We pillaged everything we could find of value, all their treasures and bits of gold and hack silver and made it ready to carry back to our ship. We cast aside their holy things and trod anything deemed worthless under foot. We rounded up what was left of these holy men, stripped them naked and decapitated them there and then in front of their altar, and the ground round about became slick with their blood.

One old monk with tonsured head and long flowing white hair came out of a side room, his hands held high in despair. Our men now had the berserk upon them and had no other thoughts other than to kill and kill again all of those that were of no value to us, but this old monk his hands still held high I suppose imploring his God to aid him, shouted out to Bjarni that the slaughter was pointless, all would arise again and even him we could not harm.

'Bring your bowmen and fire arrows into my body he called, throw your spears and hack me asunder I will show you all the power of my god and you will see that I cannot be harmed'

Bjarni stopped in his tracks and grabbed the old monk by the scruff of the neck.

'We will see about that you stupid old fool'

He called to a few of the men who had stacked their bows by the church door to bring them hither, and bade them loose their arrows at the old monk, the old boy died like the others in front of his altar, his blood mingling with the blood from his fellows already upon the flagstones.

We put several of these Christ followers to the question as to where they had hidden their holy book which we had heard so much about, Bjarni said it was known to exist in this monastery and if we could only find it, the secrets it could reveal would be only equalled by the weight of hack silver that we would receive in selling it to some rich Jarl back home. It would be invaluable he said and could tell us much about the power of their god and all his supposed secrets, many of our people were frightened of this new religion, not understanding what it was about with most not even trying to comprehend how and why it was travelling so quickly like a wildfire through a pine forest in high summer, why people were converting to this new faith and more worrying some of our own people also. If we had their book perhaps its power and secrets could be understood and we could use it to defeat these accursed white priests if we only knew what it contained. These men who followed the ways of their nailed god were like a terrible pestilence which attacked the unwary and innocent and defied the way of the true gods and like any pestilence should be wiped from the face of the earth.

We bound these monks hands behind their backs and despite us cutting their ears and lips off and gouging their eyes out, all denied the knowledge of the existence of such a book until our men lost patience with them and cut their throats and thereby sent them into the afterlife to meet their god. One other we took outside and stripped naked and Bjarni proceeded to cut his stomach open a little bit and pulled a couple of feet of his intestines out and tied it to a bush, with a little prodding from the end of someone's spear he was made to run around the bush pulling all his guts out as he went, but he would not say anything other than to howl to his god for forgiveness until he finally collapsed upon the ground and Bjarni put his spear through his chest, spitting with contempt upon the body of the unfortunate monk.

A few of the others who were young and strong had their hands bound behind their backs and we carried them back to our ships in chains. They would fetch a good price when we sold them on as slaves. If they were really lucky when we got them back to Norway they would be made slaves and thralls within our own villages, living out not to bad a life there. A few who seemed to be men of some importance amongst their own kind we also took prisoner, Arn had it in his mind to sell them back to the other White Christ believers, but if they didn't want to pay the gold we wanted, he argued we could still sell them as ordinary thralls, or cut their throats and throw them overboard if they began to be too much of a burden upon us.

There were many old and decrepit white Christ priests who blasphemed us and called us heathens and spat upon us, others kept saying they forgave us for our sin's, whatever they meant by these words we did not know, you kill your enemy you don't forgive them, forgiveness is for small children. These one's we knew were too far gone to change their ways, they would only poison the minds of whoever they came into contact with, so we took them to the edge of the cliff and cast them into the sea, screaming as they fell most dying long before they entered the sea, their bodies smashed and mangled as they were dashed time and time again against the cliff face as they fell towards the sea.

We loaded all our prisoners onboard and managed to find room for all the sacks of booty we had pillaged, most of it was silver from the ransacked monastery. We had collected weapons from the fallen enemy in the village and most of us had taken a mail shirt each from the fallen warriors bodies or from the houses that we ransacked, these mail shirts were highly sought after and they would bring in a handsome price back home. This had been a rich village and we wanted it to look like nothing but a raid from marauders coming from the sea perhaps from Friesland or Denmark. Maybe now they would be more worried about their own safety and leave our people alone, it would not take them long to figure out that the Norsemen living amongst them had not been attacked and they might wonder why, and eventually come to the correct conclusion and also perhaps have enough sense to realise that the axe wielding devils from the sea as they called us could return at any time and attack and pillage their villages once more.

We set sail as soon as we could back to the coast of Norway, slightly fearful that as we rounded the headland we might encountered a long ship or two who may be prepared to give chase and seek revenge. As it was we saw nothing other than a solitary sail on the distant horizon, which was most likely a trading knaar about its normal peaceful business.

We continued our flight back to the coast of Norway, the first few hours still had us casting the occasional fearful glance over the stern of the boat still half expecting a couple of sails to appear on the horizon and give chase, but not one materialised and we settled down deep in our own thoughts, we had made a great deal of money out of this raid, all the men already had coin and hack silver in their lockers. Arn was a fair man and we knew there would be a bit more to come from him when we sold our prisoners into slavery. A couple of the white Christ priests Arn intended to ransom back would probably bring in much gold, but this would take a bit of time to arrange, so we knew we would have to be patient.

After our raid things returned to normal, Arn found work for the boat and we settled down to the way of life that we had enjoyed before our venture across the North Sea. Arn for some reason was not quite as approachable as he had been hitherto, I just knew that he was planning something big, I just had this overwhelming feeling that he was up to something, despite this we still continued to undertake several routine voyages up and down the coast of Norway, but his mind was clearly not in it.

He was continually disappearing ashore for hours on end when we were in port, which was not his usual habit.

Chapter Six

The next time we crossed the North Sea we visited a couple of ports on the southeast coast of Wessex, it proved a successful trip from Arn's point of view to have come this considerable distance primarily to open up new trade links with these people and with future commerce now more than just a possibility. If these people were aware of an attack on the monastery and its village the previous year it was never mentioned, perhaps they were far to south for the news to have filtered down to them, most likely they would not have been particularly interested in what happened up in Scotland as we guessed there was probably not too much love lost between Wessex and the land of the Scots. Anyway it seemed to us to have no impact on the willingness of these people to want to trade with us. We then sailed up the east coast of England to Scotland putting into a remote Scottish bay prior to our return to Norway, but it was more than a little out of our way I thought and perhaps foolhardy as we had after all been raiding with Bjarni along this stretch of coast only last year. It would have made more sense to go north-westward across the North Sea and home that way.

Arn seemed to know this bay and the people here well, we had a good few items of trade goods left for sure, but it was hardly worth the effort of going out of our way to come to this place, most of the crew like me just wanted to get back to our home port.

As soon as we entered and anchored within the bay a small boat came out to us carrying a couple of men who clambered aboard, one was a young man just out of his teens who helped a much older man onto our boat. What this meeting was about nobody knew, most likely it was just to discuss our present cargo and maybe to arrange a future visit here. Arn spoke with the older man for some time and they concluded their conversation with a clasp of arms and the two of them disappeared back into their boat. A couple of our men spoke briefly with them as they cast off and rowed for the beach whence they had come.

One of the crew who was called Jarl and his brother Geirr also seemed to be familiar with this bay, it was obvious they had been here many times before, so it was not long before they had got word ashore, most likely with the younger of our now departed visitors, and it was obvious they had organised for a couple of the local whores to come aboard, Arn and Ivar realising what had passed but chose to turn a blind eye to these goings on.

Later a couple of larger boats scuttled out from the shore like pond skaters on the local mill pool, a couple of laughing girls sitting in the stern of one of them. We began almost immediately to discharge the cargo into these boats. The bay itself was fairly shallow and we could only go within a few hundred feet of the shore, or risk stranding the vessel. They would have profited from building a small quay here I though, it would have made it easier for all concerned.

The fact we still had our dragon prow in place had seemed not to alarm these people at all, most times we would stow it in the hold, long before entering these ports and bays less people get the wrong idea about our intentions, it seemed in this case Arn was using it as a signal to identify himself and his boat to these people. I think there was some history here between himself and the people living along the coast here, it was a strange feeling but Arn I had come to realise could be a bit of a mystery, especially when you thought you knew him well, he then did something out of character, but he was not the kind of man to be questioned about his past, but after all we all have our demons, which perhaps are best left sleeping.

The next morning as we ferried the two local girls ashore, Hans came sidling up to me and said

'What do you make of that boy sitting over there amongst the rocks?'

I replied

'It must be bloody cold for him; I first noticed him sitting there since shortly after dawn, he's probably the village idiot.

Hans looked at me as if I was a lump of dog's turd and turned his back on me and shuffled of across the deck in the direction of Arn who was sitting in the rear of the vessel, talking with our steersman, Hans was presumably going to ask him on his views on the boy amongst the rocks, not that Arn would be much interested I would think. Hans was getting on in years now and becoming decidedly odd in some of his ways and the remarks he made to people now and then were quite peculiar and often could be taken the wrong way, most people had enough good sense to let them go without comment, it would be imprudent to take them to seriously, or to answer Hans back as he was still handy with axe and shield, and if he had the ale or mead upon him, as often was the case, there might well be trouble, and one might not fare as well in a fight with Hans as at first you might think for, besides that all the crew knew Arn had a soft spot for him, so he was best tolerated and left alone. The death of his son a few years back in a skirmish onboard another ship, against those Dane outcasts had badly affected him, and many said he was not the man he used to be, thou if you wanted a good pair of sea boots made, then he was without doubt the best person to accomplish the task.

During the remainder of the day we made ourselves useful getting the vessel ready for the return journey back across the North sea, the tide would not return until early evening, we needed it to enable us to get over the sandbar at the entrance to this bay, more time wasted in this bay for very little gain as far as I could see, the delay made it doubly dangerous when leaving for the open sea, It was not my place to give opinions on Arn's way of doing things, it was the one thing I had found out about him, mainly from Reidar who had said to me on our very first meeting that the one thing Arn did not like, and would not tolerate from his people, his crew in particular, were those

59

who were continually in the habit of complaining about trivial things or even worse were stupid enough to criticise him. So I had made my mind up there and then all those years ago never to complain about anything to Arn, but of course what I thought about the going's on and sometimes in my opinion the stupid decisions that were made from time to time were of course a different matter. In this case I was thinking, what perhaps others were thinking also, only Odin himself knows what or who could be waiting for us when we sail out of this bay, we were not the only vessel within these waters, most would be honest traders like ourselves, but not all. As evening fell the tide turned and we made ready to sail, all of a sudden there was a bit of a commotion, Hans again I thought, I wonder what he's shouting about this time, I could hear him saying something about fishing him out of the water, I put the cable down I was coiling and wandered over to that side of the vessel the better to see what was going on, initially I thought someone had fallen over board, most Norsemen don't swim so well, so it's of concern if one of our number finds himself in the water, but it now became apparent that the village idiot we had seen amongst the rocks was living up to his name, he apparently had tried to swim out to us by all accounts and was in a bit of trouble but Bjorn had spotted him foundering in the water and was in the process of hauling him onboard by the scruff of his neck and once onboard had un-ceremonially thrown him into the ships shallow hold, to the amusement of most of the crew, except Hans who seemed more than a little perplexed. The boy looked like a half drown rat and was shivering with the cold, not surprising as he didn't even seem to have a decent cloak, and the weather was on the turn for sure, what had possessed him to swim out to our vessel, it surely was a complete mystery to me but one I was not going to spend too much time dwelling on.

After what appeared to be only a brief consultation with old Hans, we were surprised to find out that it was Arn's intention to let the boy stay onboard. Most ships captains finding themselves in this situation with an unwanted stowaway would have just cut his throat and thrown him back into the sea whence he had come, which in my opinion would have been the best course of action. It seemed the boy's name was Ranald, and that was all they knew about him. A bit on the strange side I thought at the time, but I soon put it all from my mind, there were other things to do, and now with the excitement over we were ready to sail, so pulling our stone anchor up, we hoisted the sail and made our way out of the bay and out into the open sea and back across the North sea to Norway and home.

On my return home bad news awaited me, my old grandfather had passed away just the week before, it was hardly an un-expected turn of events, as he had been of advanced years, it had upset my father more than one would have expected, with me away at sea now for extended periods and my mother who I had never really known having died when I was but a child of three or four years old, so all in all I think it had suddenly now come to him as a blow that he was all alone, as we had no other family. My mother and grandmother having both died of some kind of fever which had taken them both, and many others in the village the same winter. My father's only brother having been killed many years ago in a fight against the Danes, when the ship he was serving on had taken refuge in a fjord, perhaps to do some repairs to their vessel or escape some bad weather, and they had not noticed that there were two ships lurking nearby, and suddenly they had found themselves trapped by two Dane ships who had seen them enter into the fjord. When my uncles ship had realised their predicament they had no other recourse but to try and fight their way out of the fjord and back to the open sea which had not been without casualties, my father's brother having been one of them.

When Arn had heard of the death of my grandfather, whom he had known for many years it was his suggestion that perhaps I take some time off and stay with my father to help him come to terms with things as they now stood. I took Arn up on his offer but during my stay at my father's house, to my surprise my father did not press me once on the issue of my returning to help him on our fishing boat which I had feared he would.

There were now quite a few youths in the village now of an age when they should put aside their toy swords and shields and be given real ones, and more importantly to be taught how to use them. When my friend Bjorn was in port he could often be found down at the training ground, teaching young and not so young how to use axe and sword, he was a good teacher. It was Bjorn who came to me one day and told me to come down to the training ground the next day. He told me that he had acquired a few practice bows, reminding me that as he felt that he was not particularly good with a bow he would not necessarily be the best person to try and give the boys lessons in archery. He added that as I was now recognised as being one of the best archers in the village it might be a good idea to see if I could make passable bowmen out of some of the lads, otherwise in a few years' time he felt that we would be desperately short of warriors with these skills in the village.

Another thing Olaf he said in passing one day, I don't know if you have already heard, but that boy Ranald we picked up out of that Scottish bay has been taken in by old Hans, which seems a might odd to me. I must admit I do seem to recall that there was another Scottish man who lived with Hans and his wife for a few months before he died of injuries sustained in a sea battle or something of the like. Thou how that man's story ties in with this boy, I have absolutely no idea and even more strange I hear that Arn is apparently thinking of offering him a place on the boat, as one of the crew. As you know Ulf has already left the boat and it's also rumoured that Hans is also thinking about leaving also and staying ashore to try and make a life repairing and making sea boots and other leather things, he is not at all bad at making leather jerkins so I hear. So we may find ourselves shorthanded for the next voyage. Arn' a good judge of character, so that's enough for me, plus he's the master of the ship, so the matter is settled, but it will be a good idea to find out if the boy knows anything about the use of weapons.

So Olaf, I want you to work him hard with the bow and I will do the same with him in the use of axe and shield, he will be proficient with both shortly or I will half kill him in the attempt, we don't want to have to sail with someone who is going to let us down in the first skirmish we get involved in. If I am forced to stand shoulder to shoulder with a man in a shield wall I need to know for sure now and not later if he will stand firm and hold or not as the case may be, I don't want to find out when it's too late during a fight he's going to be the weak link in the wall. If we find a shield wall buckling because of his incompetence or worse still that we never bothered finding out if he had any skill in this direction I would feel to blame if men lost their lives because off it.

I was immensely pleased that Bjorn held me in such esteem in my capability with the bow, it seemed it was only yesterday that I was down at the training ground myself, learning how to use the axe and shield and my beloved bow, the man who had taught me in its use was still alive and lived above the village where he had a small farm, but he had given his training sessions up many years ago in favour of concentrating on looking after his farm, he was sorely missed as was now evident by Bjorn's comments. I was determined to do my best and not let Bjorn down and try to get the boys up to a good standard in the use of the bow, including our new found ship mate Ranald.

We found out later that Ranald was indeed going to be sailing on the "Sea eagle" with us, so both Bjorn and myself redoubled our efforts with him down at the training ground, it was not all charity on myself and Bjorn's part it was in our own interests and the interests of our other crew mates, that he was capable of looking after himself, and in a shield wall you needed to look out for the man either side of you also. Unfortunately it became immediately obvious to Bjorn that the boy had never welded a sword or axe in his life, so Bjorn said that there would be a great deal of work to be done with him, and quickly too as he wouldn't survive long in a fight. He's a quick learner thou and has the build to cope with using the axe well, a few years on the rowing benches will put some muscle on his shoulders and he will turn out to be at least useful to row the boat if nothing else, that is of course assuming that Ivar can teach him to row. We will also have the other problem of seeing how well our fellow Norsemen are going to tolerate a foreigner, a Scot at that, sitting at the same oars as them, it may or may not become an issue. The biggest problem for a while thou is his inability to speak our Language, I hope Hans and Arn can do something about that fairly quickly, because I for one cannot understand a single word he says.

Later that same evening when we were down at the training ground, I must admit I was pleasantly surprised, because when I gave Ranald a bow and bade him shoot some arrows each time he shot he at least he hit the bale of straw we were using as a target.

I thought he showed potential, thou the bow really does take a long time to learn to use efficiently, hours and hours of regular practice being required, so I was content with his initial showing, and thought that we will just have to wait and see how he progresses over the coming years. Most of our older youths from the village were still better than him at this stage I knew, but this was to be expected as they had started at a much earlier age and it was not of great concern to me at the moment.

I returned to Arn's boat after a few weeks, my father now being in a better state of mind, old Hans as expected did not accompany us on the next few trips, nor did Ranald, he had been left behind in order for him to try and improve his Norse and concentrate on his weapons training. Some of the voyages we were now undertaking were quite lengthy and it came as no surprise on our return to port when we heard that Han's had been telling everyone that he had given up the seagoing life for good and was staying ashore and would be concentrating on making sea boots. Perhaps it was a good decision on his part I thought when I first heard of this, he was getting on in years now and most likely had enough of ship board life. It also went some way to explain why Arn was taking a chance and about to employ Ranald to work on his boat, over the last few months we had found ourselves shorthanded as we all had expected, but it's true to say we would miss Hans for both his work and his cantankerous ways.

The following trip we returned to our home port to be greeted with the news that Hans had died, shortly after his wife had taken ill and also died. What came as a greater surprise to us all was that Ranald had inherited Hans's property and now would be joining Arn's vessel on a permanent basis. Some people have all the luck my friend Bjorn said without a trace of malice on hearing the news, he continued by saying that there was one good piece of news and that was Ranald was coming on immensely well in the use of sword and shield. He's even got his own sword now, a good quality weapon, I'm not sure where it came from, looks as if it's a Scottish blade, maybe old Han's had given it to him, it matters not other than he's getting better all the time at using it, he's been putting in a lot of time down at the training ground, plus his Norse is more or less understandable now, so things may work out with him after all.

The following spring Arn announced his long awaited decision to mount another major voyage to Iceland, a fair distance which had to be carefully balanced against whether or not our cargo and any return cargo was going to justify the time and expense for another such voyage, but Arn had been trading to Iceland for years so I doubted if he would even contemplate the trip unless he was sure of a good profit, the last voyage there had turned out well for everyone, I had filled my rowing bench locker with coin and other things which I had traded on my return home, so I was not un-happy about another trip, I liked being out in mid ocean away from land, despite being confined to a small vessel, sometimes cramped with fellow crewmen and cargo, and usually continually wet, or at least always having to sleep in damp clothes, it still gave one that feeling of absolute freedom. As we prepared the vessel in port prior to our leaving on our trip to Iceland two new men joined the crew to replace Tor and Reidar, who were leaving the vessel to join another vessel belonging to jarl Bjarni Thorfinn who was governing the lands further south down the coast. We suspected that Bjarni Thorfinn was organising a raiding trip down onto the Denmark coast, a retaliation or blood vengeance raid for atrocities committed by some Danes against his people recently. Maybe thou, some of our crew thought it was just an excuse to go raiding and to look for gold and slaves. There would without doubt probably be much booty and hack silver for the taking we suspected, and Tor and Reidar were always looking for quick money and if it involved a good fight, so much the better. Both men were capable warriors, but were probably more suited to going on raiding parties than just manning an oar on a trading knaar, they always did what was expected of them without question, but on peaceful trading voyages one sensed that they were not really happy with their lot which showed through from time to time, and it was then obvious to all that they bored of it all and wanted more excitement in their lives. Jarl Bjarni knew all of this and he also knew he would be getting two good men, he would need all he could get if he was to have the audacity to raid into the heart of the Danes homeland.

Two new crew members who joined the ship to replace Tor and Reidar were called Leif and Skeggi, both were Icelanders which brought our number of Icelanders onboard up to three now, a man called Erik having been on the vessel for some while now, and had been a replacement for my friend Ulf. Arn seemed to know the two Icelanders extremely well, and it was not just chance I think that he had employed these two, he could probably had found a couple of local men without too much effort had he so wished.

Chapter Seven

The two new crew members I took to immediately, Skeggi was easy going, quick to laugh and seemed to project the image of a casual indifference to what was going on around him but at the same time I could see that there was a much more serious side to him deep down, it was evident that he was a man who could install great confidence into the people with whom he came into contact with. I could see why Arn would want him onboard, he seemed to have a good head for business and could reason things through, but I think perhaps he never really wanted the responsibility to go further in life than what he was doing already, certainly not wanting to become master of his own boat. He had a terrible reputation for heavy drinking but having said that he was unmistakeable a warrior of some note, and as I was to find out later he would be the first to try and organise the men if something seemed about to go wrong, he would never lose his head whatever the problem was, and when it came to a fight in a tavern or brothel he seemed to have an amazing knack of sobering up instantly when it looked as if the fight could turn ugly, I never saw him provoke a fight but he certainly finished a few and came to my aid on numerous occasions when I had been stupid enough to start a ruckus. He had several silver arm rings adorning both arms. He came onboard our ship with his axe and shield a mail shirt and very little else, and for us to have a fighting man onboard such as him was a little un-usual to say the least. Most of us were not really thinking men, we didn't need to be, all we really needed were strong arms and shoulders to row ten hours a day and be able to weld axe or sword with confidence when the occasion arose. Our other new Icelander was Leif, and was a different character altogether, if there was ever such a thing as a typical Norseman then it was Leif; he was very similar in statue and attitude to my friend Bjorn. He was heavily muscled and like Bjorn had tattoos upon his upper arms and chest and you could not fail to miss the silver arm rings which adorned both arms which caught one's attention immediately, I was beginning to become quite embarrassed about my own lack of arm rings, but consoling myself with the fact that as yet I was just a sailor man, who knew how to use axe and shield to defend myself and ship, but I think the others did not yet consider me as being much of a warrior, so my lack of arm rings perhaps would not be held against me. I knew Arn did not. Leif also had heavy scars upon his chest and a bad scar upon one side of his face, thou it didn't seem to distract from his looks all that much, he was an ugly bugger to begin with, with a pox marked face, and the scar looked as if it had perhaps been earned in a knife fight. Leif had a reputation for heavy drinking and womanising, the women seemed to go for him despite his looks, and I doubt if he thought too much whether the women had husbands or not, nor probably cared, but a better man to share a rowing bench with would be hard to find.

It was only a few days sail up to Bjorgvin, the worse part of the journey would be the sail, or more likely I thought the hard row of a dozen leagues or so down into the port. Ranald our new found ship mate I had recently just found out was to be my new oar mate, Arn wanted Ivar and myself to try and make at least a passable rower out of him, it's true to say that he had the build for it and he always applied himself to the task in hand, and showed a lot of enthusiasm no matter what the task, as he did with most of the new skills that Ivar or the other crew members endeavoured to teach him, something which the others soon noticed which went quite someway in them gradually accepting him as a member of the crew. He was probably paired with me I thought because Arn knew I would not complain about the situation to much, being a fairly newcomer myself to the vessel, and in some ways still trying to prove myself to the rest of my oar mates. Most of the crew, I knew might still have some reservations about him, he wasn't Norse but it was not unknown to have men from Wessex on the oar benches of the bigger Norse boats, or even a Frank or two. Apart from all of that, it was still difficult to hold a conversation with Ranald because of his poor Norse accent, thou it was generally accepted he was improving rapidly, to the level people didn't make a joke at his expense and think he would not understand. He was easy going, but could be quick to grab his sword if he thought things had gone too far. Most of the crew instead of criticising him for lack of humour were pleased by this action.

'We will make a Norseman out of him yet'

Old Gurt had said one day after Ranald had half drawn his sword and was threatening to skewer someone for a particularly bad ribbing.

He seemed to get on well with our new Icelandic crew members, with whom he seemed to spend a lot of with, listening to what at times seemed preposterous stories of earlier voyages that they had undertook, whilst they related their stories they tried to teach him how to tie knots and splice rope. He reminded me of myself on my first real voyage, so full of enthusiasm and not wanting to miss anything, everything being so new and different in my newly adopted life, thus it was with Ranald who had us in stitches of laughter as he rushed from one side of the boat to the other as we entered the channel down to Bjorgvin, he surely didn't want to miss seeing anything. We arrived to find the port a hive of activity, I had been here several times before, with Harald and his nephew onboard the 'Starling', the port seemed to have grown in size and this time we were not the only boat tied up to the quay. The next day we starting to load cargo, in fact quite a large amount of cargo, mostly farming implements and the like, but a surprisingly large amount of weapons, with hundreds and hundreds of arrow shafts and barrels of arrow heads. A bit strange I thought at the time, I didn't think there was a great deal to hunt on Iceland, if indeed anything at all

The day before we left Bjorgvin for Iceland Skeggi and Leif went ashore, taking Ranald with them, some of us were a little surprised and disappointed that we were not also granted some time ashore, as we were about to go on a fairly lengthy voyage, but we were answered by Ivar the sailing master, who said Skeggi and Leif had business ashore to conduct on Arn's behalf, and that Arn had indicated he wanted everyone sober and we might as well get used to the idea as there was to be little drinking on the voyage across to Iceland. This caused a little bit of controversy if not a few half suppressed smiles as the two men with the worse reputations for hard drinking and whoring were the very one's Arn had sent ashore, our misgiving's seemed to be well borne out, as in the early hours there was a hell of a commotion which woke us all up, Skeggi and Leif as we had expected had returned to the ship three parts drunk, but unexpectedly we saw that they were carrying Ranald, who was completely unconscious and dead to the world. Arn gave the three of them a withering look, not that Ranald was in a condition to notice anything at all, and he then focussed on Skeggi and said

'Did you accomplish what I asked you to do before you decided to drink the town dry?'

Skeggi was looking somewhat sheepish by now, but without another word handed over a large roll of what looked like parchments or vellums, most likely they were charts I thought at the time. He then took his leave and staggered to the side of the vessel and promptly spewed over the side, much to the amusement of the rest of us.

Chapter Eight

As I remember it we left for Iceland a few days later, everyone was trying to keep out of the way of Skeggi and Leif, at least until they had recovered from their hangover and were in a better humour. Ranald I noticed didn't look so good either. He was continually spewing over the side of the ship and muttering to himself and to anyone who would listen that he had taken the pledge, ale and mead would never pass his lips again he said. We will see I thought, he would be the first man of the north yet to decline a drink and the chance to get completely legless at the first opportunity.

Things settled down on the trip into the normal routine expected onboard a vessel such as ours and we made an uneventful passage to Iceland. I had spent a lot of time in the company of Skeggi and Leif on the voyage across to Iceland either on my own or with Ranald, they confirmed to me what we all really knew, that Iceland was their homeland. They were keen to answer all my questions regarding their homeland, to relate to me the country's history, and I spent hours listening to their stories, in fact all of my off duty time, which in reality was very little whilst at sea, as there is always work to do, there was no ships master that I ever encountered allowing idleness aboard his vessel, as I had first found out when serving on the 'Starling'

I continually pestered one or other of them for yet more stories from their country. I had visited Iceland quite a few times, but had never really got to know the people there. I asked a thousand and one questions. To the surprise of myself and the rest of the crew, these men tolerated both Ranald's and my persistent questions and always answered us with good humour, despite now and then our questions most likely seeming stupid to them from time to time. I think they recognised in both of us a genuine interest in their country. They also told us all that they knew about a land that supposedly lay far to the southwest of Iceland. Slowly it began to dawn on me why these two men were onboard, originally when they had joined the vessel back in Norway we all thought that the pair of them just wanted a berth to enable them to get back home again, but it was something more, I was sure of it now. It was obvious that these two men had themselves been intrigued by the stories and accounts about this fabled land that lay to the south-west, they having listened to all of the many tales of the sightings of this mysterious land, some accounts being dismissed as nothing but over enthusiastic seamen's tales about sea witches and fetches, Cyclops and monopods. All seamen just love to spin farfetched stories to get the attention of people ashore, but the two of them had taken the time, thought about it and sifted through the information they had gained and tried to separate the make believe from fact and they were now convinced that a large land mass indeed did lie less than three hundred leagues away to the southwest. Furthermore Skeggi went on to say that they had actually glimpsed this coastline having been on a vessel blown hither and thither by a strong storm not knowing where they were and they had come into sight of a mist shrouded rocky land in the distance, they had ventured further towards this coast until they could see a green lush looking island, but the ship's captain had refused to risk his ship further and had come about and would not even entertain the idea of searching for a creek to anchor in and look for desperately needed fresh water, let along send men ashore to explore the land. So when he was sure of his bearings by the stars he turned northeast ward and with a now favourable wind he had set a course back to Iceland and safety as fast as he could.

I had thought for some months now that Arn had been planning something major and now everything was falling into place, he was going to take his ship and us in search of this land, I just knew it. Arn I had come to realise was an explorer of considerable daring, and a gambler at times when he thought the rewards justified it, but he could not by any stretch of the imagination be called reckless. Arn always sought the means necessary of ensuring that he did everything possible to put the odds in his favour when he undertook voyages to new ports and lands, and he knew by having Leif and Skeggi onboard it would give heart and courage to the rest his crew when they knew these two men had been within an arrows length of this land, that they had seen this land with their own eyes and returned home in safety and now were openly saying that they were not frightened to return a second time to explore this coastline.

We arrived in Iceland after about a month at sea, we were all of us glad to have made the passage in this relatively short time, we had been buffeted by strong winds and it had rained incessantly every day. We were all soaked to the skin and with no way of drying our clothes except to hang them up against the rigging on the mast and hope the wind did not take them. The continual motion of the boat preventing the lighting of the brazier so we could not even have hot food, instead having to make do with dried fish and meat, water had got into the bread and it was now a soggy weevil infested mess, it had been hardly edible in the first place. The whole voyage had put most of us in a foul mood and made us irritable with each other, the slightest remark made by someone however good intentioned could end up in a conflict of some description or another..

We rounded a headland and entered into the bay passing numerous small boats, usually with just one man in them or maybe two of them out in the bay checking crab pots and fishing. My mind raced back to my upbringing back at home, remembering that this was what my father had done all his life and worst still it was what he had wanted for me to do and to follow in his footsteps as he had continued what his father had started before him. I thanked my long dead grandfather now for speaking up on my behalf to my father and making him see it from my point of view, that fishing was not what I was born to do.

We came alongside the quay, tying our vessel up behind a large knaar, that was riding high in the water and looked like she was almost finished discharging her cargo and would be setting sail in the next few days.

Almost as soon as we were alongside the usual amount of honest traders and riffraff scuttled across the boarding plank no sooner than we had placed it from ship to dock, they reminded me of rats scurrying up a mooring line looking for a better life than what they were having in the shore side warehouses.. Two men immediately sought Arn out. He ushered them to a quiet place at the rear of the vessel to conduct their business, sitting on barrels and taking the occasional swig of mead out of a skin that one of them had produced. They left apparently happy and a short while later several carts arrived and lined up upon the quay. A group of men, who had been huddled against the weather in groups upon the quay, waited to board our vessel and to start the work of discharging our cargo into the waiting carts. Standing under the arch of a warehouse door I notice a group of women and young girls sheltering as best they could against the now quite persistent rain, a bit of rain was not going to stop the local girls from plying their wares. Several other carts began to arrive and bring their contents onto our ship, a lot of it seemed to be food; a fresh side of beef and a lot of barrels, probably containing salted fish and pork, and possibly ale; some sacks of grain and also a few crates appeared, which, considering the squawking and honking coming from them, contained live ducks and geese. A couple of live sheep made their appearance and bleated pitifully, as they were stowed on board, probably already guessing the fate which awaited them. I was a bit disappointed at this sight, all of this fresh food just signified to me that Arn was having the ship stored strait away in readiness for a quick turn around and back to our homeland again. But as the day progressed, and having little to do, I observed that there was as much being brought onto the ship as was being removed into the shore side carts. Also I noticed a lot of our outward cargo was not being sent ashore, now this was indeed a might odd I thought at the time.

Arn, not unexpectedly to my mind in retrospect, called a meeting of all the crew, we were all by now suspecting something was afoot. Arn had expressly forbidden anyone to go ashore until he had a chance to speak to all of us. So as we stood there assembled in the well of the ship, behind a canvas dodger trying to keep the wind and rain from ourselves Arn began by outlining his intentions of trying to find the uncharted land that lay far to the south west of Iceland, this land that had been seen countless times, but no one had as yet made landfall on or even tried to explore this land mass. A land that was known to be green and lush, a land that was long overdue to be explored by men of courage and adventure such as ourselves. He turned and pointed at Leif and Skeggi and said

'See these two men here before you, they have already seen this land, with their own eyes this is where I propose to take us all to explore this land and see what it holds, now listen lad's any of you not wanting to accompany me can say so now and I will release you from the oath that binds you to me and none will think the worst of you. You can go ashore and find another berth to get yourselves back to Norway and I will give you money for your pocket as well, so you will not feel you have had a wasted trip'

Not one man moved except old Borg who as usual at these meetings always had to have his say, he was a grizzled old warrior of advancing years and now he started to mumble something about all the vessels that had left Norway bound for Iceland and thence back to Norway not all had made it into their home ports; in fact many were never to be seen again. Were the bones of these boats and their crews lying white and bleached upon this distant shore, he asked? Borg continued by saying that perhaps what Arn was suggesting was not such a matter-of-fact journey as he was trying to make it out to be. Arn soon silenced Borg, suggesting that perhaps he should remain in Iceland and get himself a wife and hang up his axe and shield if he was not up to this adventure. This soon silenced Borg, he knew already as well as Arn and the rest of us he would be coming on this voyage. Despite his brusque and cantankerous nature Borg was well liked and admired by all his oar mates. His prowess with a battle axe was legendary. Borg eventually ended the conversation himself by saying that he would go and look for his country men's bones on this distant shoreline if there were any to be found, and his bones could join them if that was to be the way of things.

'Just as long as my sword is in my hand he said, so that when I go to sit with Odin in the great hall of Valhalla, he does not think me unworthy of my place at his table'

Our meeting over the crew dispersed, most went straight ashore with Arn's warning about careless talk and getting into drunken brawls still ringing in their ears. I looked around the ship, all was more or less in order but I still stayed onboard for a couple of hours or more just fussing over this and that checking and rechecking that all was stowed correctly and as it should be, re coiling a rope that didn't need it, checking barrels were tightly roped against the ships rail and all manner of other things. My antics must have attracted Arn's attention because presently he came over to me and said

'Time you went ashore yourself Olaf; there's not much to do here for a while not until we sail at least, I would think we are all stowed away as good as we can be, the shore side boys will look after the ship for us and check the bow and stern lines periodically. It's going to be a long time before we can enjoy the company of women again and be able to take a drink or two in a relative civilised place. So get yourself up to that tavern behind the fish ware house and get yourself a mug of ale or two. I will join you presently.

I checked that I had a couple of coins and a small piece of hack silver in my pocket and went down the solitary plank that served as our gangway. I wandered the short distance through the maze of filth strewn streets to the tavern. I had to duck my head as I entered through the low door way and into the tavern, which smelt just as bad inside as it did outside in the streets. The taverns close proximity to the fish warehouse not helping things too much in that direction. As I entered the establishment I could see that there was already about a dozen of our crew already in the far corner of the room, they had a remarkable talent for getting themselves three parts drunk in quite a short space of time, they had not let me down today in that respect, it never ceased to amaze me. I ignored their call for me to join them, instead as I had seen old Gurt sitting at a table by the window adjacent to the rickety bar I made my way across the room to join him. He seemed in deep conversation with a man I did not recognise, probably just a local man out for a drink himself. The bar keep brought a couple of jugs of ale and another mug over to the table, the three of us passed a leisurely hour or so talking about this and that, mainly about farms and crops and the like, it seemed that our companion had a small farm up in the hills and had come to town to do a bit of business and have some time to himself. Gurt himself was really more farmer than warrior and it was refreshing for me to sit and listen to such simple and safe conversation for a while.

Presently Arn entered the tavern paused for an instant in the doorway and looked around, seeing the three of us seated at the table made a bee line for us, the bar keep throwing him an empty tankard as he made his way across the room. He seated himself on a stool opposite Gurt and I sitting next to the local man, his back to the rest of the room, and in response to a wave of my hand in the direction of the of jug ale he pour himself a mug of the foaming ale.

Shorty there was a commotion and much good-natured laughter coming from the far side of the room which had the four of us instinctively looking over to the other side of the room to see the source of it all.

We saw that Ranald had one of the serving wenches on her back spread eagled over the table his breeks around his ankles with several of his crew mates encouraging him to greater endeavours.

Arn shook his head as he turned back to us saying

'In the name of Odin what happened to that quiet lad we found in that Scottish bay all those years ago. He's become worse than any of them, and for Odin's sake look at that wench, she's got a face like a pickled trout. Old Hans and his wife Hilda would likely turn in their graves if they knew how he carried on now, it's high time that we were away from this place now I want to feel the movement of my boat under my feet again with the wind and rain in my face, I have had my fill of civilisation for a while it's time we were back looking for whatever lies there across the western ocean.

Chapter Nine

Two days later after an all but to short time ashore we returned to our boat, with a few of the crew nursing major hangovers, having under estimated the strength of the local ale and imported mead, which was nothing short of evil. We left Iceland bound for the tip of Greenland to get one last accurate position before turning south west for the three hundred league sail towards where we expected to find the northern coast of the New found land, as it generally seemed to be known as now

Five days later having made remarkably good time we arrived in the vicinity of the southern tip of Greenland it occurred to me that a few years earlier I had heard that a few hundred settlers had left Norway with the intention of founding a settlement on the sheltered southwest coast of Greenland, but nothing had been heard from them for years. None had returned, and worse still no one had followed them, or indeed even tried to resupply them. Arn confided to me that he had toyed with the idea of sailing up the coast of this land to see if he could find their settlement and see if any of the settlers had survived, but had thought better of it, not wanting to waste the time and perhaps have to get involved in these people's problems if things were not as they should be, we both thought that it was more than likely that there was nobody or anything left to find anyway. That of course was making the assumption they had actually reached their destination in the first place and that their ships had not foundered on the voyage across from Iceland. If they had indeed managed to found a settlement there it would have been hard to survive that first winter and by now maybe all were dead from hunger or disease. It was thought that there would be no trees growing in this barren land even on this sheltered southwest coast so they would have had a problem with fuel for their fires and would have had perhaps to sacrifice their boats to supplement the timber they had brought with them to build their shelters. They must have been a desperate or foolhardy people to even have thought that it was feasible to survive in that land, they must have known that it was a one-way voyage. I could only marvel at their determination and hope that all went well for them and that they have survived and flourished.

So with these grim thoughts put to the back of our minds, we had used the tip of Greenland as our last known landmark and continued on our way southwest in search of land. I suppose it would be true to say that there was some trepidation existing in most of our minds as to what would happen on this path Odin had put us on

Arn was sure now that we would encounter this new land within the week, dependent on us encountering some good winds and favourable currents, least wise that's what he had told the crew back in Iceland. Privately to me he told me that we were taking a huge gamble, a gamble with our lives, we knew there was land out there, but its exact location still remained a mystery to everyone, and he further confided in me that we knew nothing of the winds or currents and if this land turns out to be an island and we miss it we will sail on until we run out of water and food I noticed he didn't say until we sail of the edge of the world. Arn was an enlightened navigator and just refused to listen to the old fishwives tales as he put it that claimed the world was like a tortoise's back and one had to be careful and not sail to far over the horizon and come to its edge and disappear into the vortex below it. He often during our long talks about navigation spoke of the curvature of the ocean and how you could observe a ships mast disappearing when it got as far as the horizon, not because of it being beyond our sight but because of this curvature of the ocean. Arn emphasized the need to find this land, it was absolutely critical that we resupply ourselves for the voyage back home; otherwise we will most likely find ourselves starving to death on some bleak distant shore all hope gone and nothing to do but sit there and await the end. Many had claimed to have seen this land, we had two such men onboard with us now, and several reputable ships captains personally known to myself have reported a large landmass to the southwest of Greenland, we have all been hearing these stories for years and I truly believed that they are true, I have weighed the risks up and I am now of the mind that it's worth the gamble, the land is there we just need to find it. Many its true have found this land by accident when blown of course on voyage from Norway to

Iceland. Yet it's still unbelievable to my mind that as yet no one has ever tried to go back to seek this land out again and chart it, most were I suppose just thankful that they were able to come about once the storm had abated and make their way back to Iceland and live to tell their tale.

We sailed ever in a south-westward direction, the weather was fine, it was late summer, or least ways was back in our own land. But then the weather began to turn, some days still warm but then sudden squalls appeared from nowhere, the current was strong and by our reckonings we were being steadily driven north westward to who knows where. One evening I was in the stern of the vessel talking to Arn who was seated on a stool sitting in front of a large barrel he was using as a make shift table. Suddenly the oarsman pointed towards the lantern that Arn was trying to study his charts by, it took a second for Orrn's meaning to become clear, and then it dawned on the pair of us like somebody had thrown a bucket of cold water over us both to waken us. The light from the lantern had attracted dozens of moths and what looked like flies, but what they were was a mystery to us as we had nothing to match them back home. However It could mean only one thing, land and we were close into it by my reckoning.

The next morning instead of us sighting the land that was so obviously close by, the heavens opened up and there was such a deluge of rain that few of us had encountered before. The wind rose with alarming force and buffeted us with such force we thought the mast would be ripped out of its block, even thou the sail had been taken in several hours ago. Thor showed no mercy towards Tanngrisnir and Tannngnjostr as he urged them ever onwards across the darkening western sky, the lighting was splitting the skies asunder and as he wielded his battle hammer the sound of thunder became unbearable and turned our men's bowels to water.

We were being slowly but surely pushed more and more north westward away from what we believed to be our New found land. The wind blew with such tremendous force that we thought that we were all destined for a watery grave, borne out when suddenly there was a tremendous cracking sound and the ship shuddered and we all looked up in horror to see that the top section of our mast had sprung, it still held but the damp furled sail had sagged and had conspired with the wind aiding in its demise, it was obvious the mast could not support it any longer. Whatever place it was that we were being pushed towards by this storm we now knew we would have to except, whatever land that Loki had chosen as our destination us we would need to embrace if we wanted salvation. Odin willing we might be able to beach the vessel and make repairs and be thankful that we had managed to make a landfall at all. With the break of dawn and the morning showing herself in full splendour we could now see that we had been swept into a huge bay, several miles across and the same deep, we could see two headlands either side of us, in front of us was a shelving shale beach, with trees in places growing to a few hundred feet of the shore line. We unshipped our oars and rowed in close to the shore, the men putting their backs into the task, anxious now to feel solid ground under their feet, the bow almost grounding on the shelving beach. We dropped our stone anchored over the side, still being a few dozen feet from shore, the bottom seemed sound so a couple of the men slid over the side and waded ashore and hammered into the shale beach a couple of mooring stakes, as we were not completely sure that the anchor would hold.

It was still heavily overcast but at least the rain had now ceased and the wind had abated considerably. We felt the boat was safe now so we set about discussing what our next options were, and the best way to proceed and find a way out of the predicament we now found ourselves in. We realised that we would have to replace the mast, it might be repairable Guilli our ships carpenter thought, well at least back at home it would be, but here it might be nigh impossible he said perhaps it would be better to replace the entire mast, at least then we would be able to trust that it will not splinter again. Thus the decision was forced upon us; we would have to stay somewhere on this coast line and repair the vessel, with the summer coming to an end in a few months' time it would most likely make it necessary for us to winter over on this coast somewhere. At least it would give us the chance to explore on foot some of the country side and see what was here, the beach here was not looking particularly promising. We looked around and quickly came to the conclusion that perhaps this was not an ideal spot to make our basecamp and build a stockade, even though we were in a bay we could see that it was far to exposed to the open ocean. We would most likely have to venture inland if we wanted to build a stockade to provide ourselves with shelter and give ourselves some place we could defend if the situation arose, but this would then leave us with no option but to leave the boat anchored out in the bay, or beach her and have her laying on an exposed beach all through the winter. If there were people already living here in this land, and there was we thought a good chance that this would well be the case, with our boat thus exposed it would be in full view of any passing Skraelings. Nobody needed to have it spelled out to them we all knew full well that losing the boat would sign our death warrants.

We were on a journey of exploration, so we all knew now it would take several years or more before we could return home, it was not a problem we didn't really think or speak about home all that much anyway, we were here doing what we had come to do and there were not any complaints from the men, especially as we were now ashore and safe with the prospect of fresh food and water being available shortly, a thing that was upper most in the minds of most of us.

If we had to stay in this land during the coming winter months before continuing with our journey, from what we had seen already of it, this was not deemed to be such a problem, the land here was no different from our lands back home, perhaps as good or even better we thought. We risked a fire to cook what remained of our food and most of the men took the opportunity to try and dry their clothes. At the moment we had no reason to think that we were in any kind of danger, our boat was close at hand and we could soon put out into the bay to escape to another part of the coast if needs be. It was uppermost in our minds this land could well be inhabited by other people, but we thought it unlikely they would stumble across us strait away, and even if there were people here, it was such a vast country maybe they would leave us alone and go about their own business and leave us to ours unmolested.

The very next day we were about to realise how wrong we had been with this line of reasoning. During the night we had heard strange calls coming from the forest which we could not identify, but as we had also heard the cries of wolves snapping and snarling at each other over a nearby kill, something that we were familiar with we thought not too much of it at the time, although admittedly it unsettled a few of us, me included.

The next day Skeggi and a lad called Cnut went up the beach away to explore and look for shell fish and crabs amongst the rocks, they had been told by Arn to stay on the beach, or at least not to stray too far into the tree line. The peace of the morning was shattered a few hours later when we heard shouts from up the beach, it took a few seconds for it to register as to what was happening. We could see that Skeggi and Cnut staggering out of the tree line and it soon appeared to all that Cnut was injured. We could see even from this distance an arrow protruding from his chest. Old Borg was the nearest to them, and was quicker than the rest of us to react to the situation. He turned to us and bid us all stay where we were, Arn picking up on the situation immediately and ordered us to form a defensive position and be ready to form a shield wall if thought necessary. Borg loped of up the beach in support of his two comrades, almost as soon as he had come up to Skeggi and Cnut, out of the forest came a dozen or so Skraelings in pursuit of them. Borg put himself between the Skraelings and his two comrades and we could faintly hear him yelling at Skeggi to get Cnut back to the safety of the ship and our makeshift encampment further down the beach. Borg had been up the beach looking for driftwood and so had his double headed battle axe with him, he stood waiting we thought to see what the Skraelings would do and also to give time for Skeggi to carry Cnut back to safety. The two of them had almost made it back to us when we suddenly became aware of there being more Skraelings in the tree line near to us, the primitives launched a hail of arrows in the direction of Skeggi and Cnut, Cnut was hit yet again by another arrow and Skeggi staggered and fell hit by at least three arrows and the pair of them slumped to the ground. Our own archers including myself responded and shot at the shadows in the tree line, meanwhile Leif ran out from the safety of our group to aid his friend, two other men quickly followed him and Skeggi and Cnut were dragged back to the comparative safety of our makeshift camp site. Skeggi was already dead and it was evident that Cnut was badly injured.

Further down the beach, we watched in horror as Borg stood his ground, despites shouts from Arn to retreat back towards us and we would try to keep the Skraelings at bay with our own archers, but it was not to be the way of things, before Borg could take further action the Skraelings charged him. Borg fought like one of Odin's own, and he never retreated so much as an inch, retreat was not in old Borg's vocabulary, he cleaved several of the Skraelings limb from limb with his axe, but they were all over him and we had to watch on in horror helpless to do anything as he was eventually overcome by the Skraelings who beat him to death with their primitive stone axe and clubs. Within minutes the Skraelings disappeared back into the forest, to regroup or await more men was unknown to us at this time.

Meanwhile we had propped Cnut up against our boat, he would not tolerate us laying him down, and for the rest of the day and throughout the coming night he choked and gurgled his life away, without us being able to do anything more for him. We had removed the arrow, but it must have pierced a lung, the second arrow had lodged in his thigh and was of no consequence compared to the one in his chest. Poor Cnut, he had known very little about fighting Skraelings or anyone else for that matter. He boasted no mail shirt, or any other body armour, except an old shield that somebody had given him, and an ancient, battered leather skullcap, with an equally neglected rusting sword that he never attended to which probably never mattered anyway as he was completely inept at its use, never having had much training. I recall that Bjorn had continually tried to improve his ability in the use of sword and shield, going over the same moves time and time again in the few practice sessions that time allowed for, but Cnut was no warrior. He had hailed from Iceland, and had joined us for adventure and to make his fortune. I remember him back in Iceland, a freed slave, who had been owned by a man who had converted to the teachings of the white Christ, and who now thought it wrong to own another fellow being as a slave, and thus had set him free. I can remember how happy Cnut was when Arn ordered Guilli to remove his slaves collar, telling him he could accompany us on our voyage if he so wished. The boy himself had recently converted to the new faith and had been baptised back in Iceland, a free man for the first time in his life. He might not have been much of a fighting man, but he could recite a lot of our favourite Norse sagas and he could sing well and was always of cheerful disposition despite the cold and damp conditions on the boat. The lack of decent food and all the other problems that were a fact of daily life on one of our long ships, all he endured without complaint, which meant that he was well liked. Despite his failings as a warrior he was accepted as one of the crew. He rowed well and that was good enough for most of us. Although we knew him to be a Christian he never spoke of it and we never saw him praying to his new god, his religion and beliefs were never mentioned amongst the crew, despite the fact that he knew we had killed many white Christ priests back in Scotland he never held it against us. There were many now who sought the protection of the old and the new religions, we thought that he was one of them and so we left him be.

We built a huge funeral pyre at the edge of the shore and placed Skeggi and Borg's body on it, along with their weapons and with their shields covering their bodies. Their other possessions stored in their row benches which doubled as a locker would be shared out amongst us later that evening. It was debated now amongst us as to how we should send Cnut on his final journey, whether it should be alongside his comrades Borg and Skeggi, or as Haggard was insisting, that of giving him a Christian burial.

'I shared an oar bench with him for a few months, he rowed well, never complained about anything and was good company, I suppose it's true to say that we became friends of sorts. As long as my sword is in my hand when I die so I can go and sit at Odin's table in the afterlife, I don't much care what happens to my body, I am not much for religion, even our own, but I think Cnut would have liked to go to his new god in the way of their people'

Arn listened and nodded his consent, so it was settled. We set fire to Skeggi and Borg's funeral pyre and sent them on their way to the afterlife to sit at the great table in the hall of Valhalla, to drink and feast and tell outrageous stories of their exploits in life, until the long awaited call came for all men of worth to muster and fight in that one last fateful battle that all would know already that they could not win.

We buried Cnut as deep in the ground as we could manage up on a rise overlooking the bay, where he could keep a look out for the return of his countrymen one day perhaps. Haggard fashioned a wooden cross out of a couple of large pine trunks, that when finished stood head and shoulders higher than a tall man. We had buried Cnut as deep in the ground as we could so that nothing would disturb his slumber and then we placed the cross above Cnut's body, it seemed strange because in the past we had all killed Christians and their accursed white Christ priests, but not one person said anything about the way we sent Cnut on his final voyage.

We now realised that we must leave this Loki cursed beach and row out into the bay and round the headland we could see in the distance and search for somewhere more secure where we could put into and repair the ship properly, and equalling important with the coming of the winter, we would need to build some shelters for ourselves. Some of our men, especially Ranald who had held Borg in high esteem wanted revenge on the Skraelings for their comrade's deaths but Arn said no to this. Even thou he expected the Skraelings would be back soon he said we could not risk another confrontation. It was more disconcerting when we knew we had not come to this land to fight, but only to explore and trade if possible with any Skraelings we came across. That was all behind us now for sure I thought. The decision to stay in these lands for the winter was forced upon us and all too soon we knew we would presently be seeing the snow geese high above us and hear their honking as they flew southward for the winter.

Chapter Ten

With a backward glance up at Cnut's grave we manned our oars and slowly rowed across the bay for a distance of perhaps five leagues or so. We presently came up to an island that was well within the bay itself, situated to our right. We couldn't really see any suitable landing places, but as we considered we were still not far enough away from the beach which had cost us dearly, so we decided to follow the islands eastern shoreline, thus estimating the island to be about two leagues long. We continued rowing, not really being able to make any use of the sail due to the condition of the mast. We continued for what we guessed to be about a further three leagues or so, and reached a large, forested island. We could see a group of smaller islands to the left and much further out we could see the open ocean. To the right of this island was what we took to be the mainland. Although still relatively early we decided to get close into the main island and anchor for the night, intending to make an early start the next day. Arn after much discussion with myself and the other men he had decided to look for a well sheltered headland or peninsular or perhaps even better a small island on which we could build some shelters and a stockade which we could defend against the Skraelings if the situation arose. We hopefully could winter over in safety and be in an area that would provide us with easy access to the surrounding forests and rivers when we needed to venture out hunting and to gather wood, but at the same time it would need to be a place to where we could return quickly at any sign of danger. We mainly feared a land launched attack, we thought that these Skraelings could well have boats of some description but not ones able to cause us to much concern, we felt it was most unlikely they would be able to launch an attack on us from the bay or the open sea. We may well have been thinking this thou in ignorance and our arrogance telling us that we were the better seamen.

But one thing was sure only an island or peninsula would really suit our needs, if such a place could be found. We were too few in numbers to defend an encampment from all four sides.

We started the next day as soon as dawn first showed herself upon the horizon, rowing in a northeast through the channel with the mainland to our right, Arn said he had a hunch that this would prove to be a large area of land jutting out towards the ocean, based on the theory that as we had just left a bay it was conceivable there was a series of bays and inlets all the way down the coast. After several hours of following the coastline we anchored once more in the shallows, no more than a hundred yards off the coast. Arn then decided to put three of our men ashore so that they could explore the area on foot, if he was right about there being numerous bays down the coast line we could sail for days and not come to a decision as to which was the better place to set up a winter base. So he thought it best to explore this section on foot and see just how far this land extended. Arn chose a couple of reliable men for the task and they lowered themselves over the side of the vessel and waded ashore and up the beach with no mishap and quickly disappeared into the fairly sparse woodland.

Later in the day when they returned they reported that although they had not travelled the entire distance across this landmass but that they had ventured far enough to see the ocean on the other side, a distance of no more than three leagues distance. This was welcome news; it showed we had found the peninsular we sought with ocean on three sides. Our men told us that they had seen no evidence of habitation or any sign of passing Skraelings. More importantly they said they had seen from a small rise, what looked like a small inlet, with a shelving stone beach on one side and heavily wooded on the other side. They went onto say that they had seen many indications of game having recently been in the vicinity, having seen the droppings of deer and also seeing many partridge and other fowls in the area, including some large black and white birds, with bright red wattles, which when startled, made a curious gobbling type sound, birds that were completely unknown to them surmising they were just indigenous to these new lands that we now found ourselves in.

We spent the night anchored once again, stirring early the next morning at first light, keen to resume the exploration of the coastline. We wanted to find the creek that our scouts had reported as soon as we could, we rowed up the coast a few leagues, coming to the headland and rowed across its northern coast, then when we altered course to the south we were soon able to confirm that we had indeed found what we sought, a peninsula of sorts with a creek all but separating it into an island which looked as if it would serve our needs. We considered ourselves sufficiently far away now from the Skraelings that we had encountered within the bay. This place had the potential of being a safe haven for us, and with the winter encroaching quickly upon the land we thought it was unlikely the Skraelings would want to venture as far as this just in search of us, soon they would most likely have other things on their minds, winter was not a time to wage war. We found the inlet that our scouts had observed on their cursory survey of the land and rowed maybe a half mile up the shallow river and found a promising looking place that seemed as if it would fulfil our needs. Thus the decision was made that we would build our stockade here up above the stone and shingle beach. The forest here was quite sparse and would give us a good view of any approaching Skraelings from behind us. We thought it would be a good idea to utilise the trees from the opposite bank to build our stockade and shelters, and that we could float them across the river as it was not very wide and only a few feet deep. It would also give the added benefit of clearing the land in front of us, and would deny the Skraelings the opportunity to encroach upon us un-noticed. We would have a good beach here to drag the vessel up onto as Guilli thought it would be a good idea to get her out of the water for the winter months. It would also be a good opportunity to make any necessary repairs to the hull and then we could refloat her come the spring and anchor her out in mid channel until we were ready to resume our journey.

We were split into various work groups to attend to the numerous tasks that urgently needed our attention. Arn gave me and Gurt the task of going out into the forest to look for game. A number of men were also sent into the forest to fell the trees needed to build the stockade, most of the tree logs that needed to be harvested would not necessarily have to be that big, especially the ones destined for use in the building of our cabins, so the work was expected to progress fairly quickly. Leif and a couple of the other men had been given the task of finding a suitable pine tree that we could use for our replacement mast. It took them a couple of days, but they eventually returned with a fine-looking pine trunk. They had already trimmed it and cut it to more or less the right length to make it more easily handled when carrying it back to the stockade. The rest of the men with some ship building skills were left to do repairs upon the vessel. We hoped that during the logging operation there would be no Skraelings close by out on a hunting trip, who would hear the noise from the tree felling and come to investigate the source of it. We wanted no further confrontation with the primitives, or at least not until our stockade was built, and we were in a position to defend ourselves.

Gurt and I having been instructed by Arn to go abroad and hunt for deer or whatever else we could find, so we took our bearings and ventured into the forest both of us glad of a break from work and the company of the others. Gurt had been with Arn periodically for many years, not exactly a young man any more, he had a farm back home, but he said that he could do with some money to develop it further, mainly to replace livestock he had lost in an exceptionally cold winter a couple of years back. He had expressed his wish to Arn to be allowed this one last adventure, before he got too old to go to sea again, which was why he had jumped at the chance of coming on this voyage when he knew where we were going in the hope of this one last chance available to him to make his fortune, if not that at least he would get to see a distant a hitherto unexplored land. He had left a wife and two grown sons on the farm. His wife had got used to him being away for months on end when he was at sea, but this voyage would be the longest he had ever been away from home he said and he now worried about his farm and family, and I secretly expected he would be happy for us to return back to Norway after the winter and not go exploring further into the unknown. We were about to turn about and head back towards the river and try our luck in that direction in our search for game, when I saw a movement in the trees, followed by the noise of a twig snapping in the undergrowth. Gurt heard the noise at the same time as me and putting his finger to his lips bade me be quiet and then I saw him knock an arrow to his bow. It was a deer close by that had got his attention, it briefly showed itself; a magnificent looking stag with large antlers it paused just an instant too long before taking flight. Gurt loosed his arrow which found its mark just behind its left shoulder, driving into the beast at an angle and into its heart. It moved forward a few feet and collapsed onto its front legs, blood spurting from its nostrils. We rushed over towards the doomed beast and I quickly finished the job with my seax. I disembowelled the beast putting the heart and other offal into a sack and then we tied the deer's legs together and slung the deer on a spruce pole which Gurt had cut and in this fashion we carried it back towards the river, being glad the distance was not too far, as the deer weighted heavily upon our shoulders by the time we had made it to the river bank. The logging operation continued for several days, but as sufficient logs became available to justify it, the men hitherto engaged on ship repairs were taken off this task and started building the cabins to shelter us during the coming winter months. One long house was proposed and two smaller buildings, one for Arn and the senior men, another split into two rooms to act as cook house and store room, and the long house for accommodation for the rest of us.

A few days later the rest of the men started building the palisade that would protect us from any attack from the Skraelings, and to serve to stop any wild animals from straying into the camp, attracted by the smell of food or plain curiosity. We suspected that as the land was similar to our homeland there may well be bears in the vicinity, perhaps not yet gone into hibernation, if indeed they acted the same as our bears did back home. We knew already there was an abundance of wolves in the forest, hearing them calling to each other nightly. Work progressed quickly and Arn eventually relaxed the pace of operations, giving everyone time away from work, a few men at a time allowing them to go hunting and fishing enabling us to have surplus meat and fish which we could smoke and dry, to tide us over for a few days if the weather set in with a vengeance and we were unable to go out hunting. It was not too long before the stockade was complete, an elevated watch tower at one corner of the rectangular palisade and a small gate allowing perhaps four men abreast to enter at a time. It could be secured when closed from within by a heavy log giving further protection against our enemies. We had a few short days of comparative calm, our stockade and buildings completed. The weather gradually drew colder, with heavy frosts in the early mornings followed by bright clear days. It started with occasional rain, which turned to sleet and then one morning we awoke to find about a foot of snow upon the ground. It snowed incessantly for days, until several feet of it lay upon the ground, confining us to our stockade. Despite our enforced confinement by the weather we were happy with the turn of events. At least we felt secure from discovery or any attack from the Skraelings. We still found plenty of things to do within the stockade and inside our buildings. On the better days we were able to send out small hunting parties in several directions. They invariably came back with something or another. On the really good days it would be a deer, or sometimes just fowls of the air. The strange sounding black and white birds made excellent eating when we could find them., We found them quite easy to hunt and bring down; they seemed to have little fear of man. We also ventured out onto the frozen river and broke holes through the ice and caught fish in this manner, just the same as we did back home, but it was a major problem for us now that we had exhausted all our grain and were unable to make fresh bread, we had quite a bit of bread left, but it was as hard as rock as it was made only of flour and water with a bit of salt added and now to our frustration it had become infested with weevils. Notwithstanding a few problems, as the months progressed we reflected during the long winter evenings spent indoors that things were not going too badly. The land here was good, plenty of timber and plenty of game within the forests, with fish in the river and in the nearby ocean. The winter would be hard here we knew, but we were use to it, and it would most likely be no worse than back at home. The winter progressed, and we all settled into a kind of routine. Men were still doing improvements on the stockade, notably to the buildings within it, even though we knew our stay here would be but brief, and we hopefully would be on our way within three or four months. The work that we were now doing on the buildings within the palisade was just perhaps something to keep ourselves occupied, something Arn and myself encouraged, we didn't want the men to become bored with all the problems that that could bring with a lot of people living together in close proximity. Thou it's true to say that the improvements we made to our living quarters were most welcome. We repaired clothes and weapons and on the brighter days we went out to the vessel to do some work on our ship. Caulking the seams with tar and moss, and checking this and that, but the cold soon drove us back into the warmth of the buildings. Our new mast had been brought inside our longhouse after a few weeks seasoning outside in the compound. Guilli was a fair carpenter and he had removed the bark from the trunk and smoothed over any knots with an adze and then painstaking went over the entire mast, until it was completely smooth. Some of the other men set to repairing the sail, sewing in new cleats and rings. They then turned their attention to repairing the rigging, using new rope. The old mast had already been removed from its block a few days earlier and everything was in place to fit the new mast. With a bit of ingenuity and as it turned out with the considerable experience Guilli was able to offer in this direction, we managed to get our new mast in its block, well secured and solid. Arn pronounced he was well pleased with our efforts and thought that we should not have problems with it when we hoisted the sail and were ready to continue on our journey.

A few weeks later the thaw set in, there were a few false starts, but slowly the snow melted, the ice on the river breaking into chunks and being forced down stream to the open ocean by the force of the current, stronger than usual due to the melt water flowing from the land and into the river. Buds appeared upon the trees and bushes, geese were flying northwards once more honking as they went, all of it being a good sign that winter was over and it lifted our spirits considerable Now the spring was rapidly encroaching upon us, it became easier to move around the forest during our hunting trips, nothing was openly said, but the men now became more cautious as they travelled along the game paths in the forest as they pursued deer and other creatures for the pot. If it was easier for us to be travelling along the forest paths, so it would be for the Skraelings. We were now greatly concerned that we could be discovered by them as they ranged through their forests on hunting trips of their own. The time had come to leave our palisade and continue our voyage of discovery. We already had the boat in the water, anchored midstream, so we finished loading her with all the things that we deemed necessary for our voyage, and a few days later we left the safety of our stockade by the creek and rowed down towards the open sea to resume our exploration of the coast that lay to the south.

We set sail in a southern direction following the coast, passing many inlets and many small islands to our right. We slowly began to appreciate the immensity of this new land that we had discovered. Most nights we anchored in shallow waters in the lee of an island. Other evenings we took a chance and ventured a short distance up an inlet or river, securing the vessel to a tree, or used our mooring poles, hammered into the beach or river bank by our axes, ever watchful for signs of Skraelings. The fishing was good and we had no problems finding small game. Occasionally we saw seals basking on the shoreline or floating on their backs, eating a recently caught fish, or just singing their unique song to each other. When the opportunity arose we took a seal or two, which were always welcome. Any meat or blubber left over we dried as best we could for leaner times, the blubber we rendered down in a large cauldron overnight so we had oil for lamps and to use for cleaning our weapons and mail to stop them from going rusty. On other occasions we saw the water spout from the blowholes of large barnacle-encrusted whales. This surely was a land of plenty.

We knew we had no hope of exploring this land and all its islands in one short summer; it would take years to realise the full potential and fully explore this coastline, but we decided to venture on for a few more weeks. We sailed ever southward, finding food and fresh water was never a problem, we didn't encountered any more Skraelings, or for that matter during our excursions ashore did we ever see any evidence of the land here having being occupied by them. If they did live in any numbers in this land then it was away from the coast deep in the forests or whatever lay further inland. We sailed up several rivers, one river we sailed up for the best part of two days taking a chance that we would not be seen by any hostile Skraelings who would then try to impede our return back down the river to the sea. One day we saw a small herd of bison, similar beasts to what some of us had seen either in our own lands or on our voyages to other distant lands. I had never seen such animals and I was over awed at their size. Several of the men went ashore and circled unnoticed around them and were able bring one of the animals down.

We saved the pelt, it was huge and back home it would bring a handsome price. We fed well for several days on the meat and what we could not eat we set about smoking over a fire, but we were reluctant to stay too long in the area accomplishing this task, ever fearful of being discovered by Skraelings once more. So we returned down the river unmolested and back into the open sea and once more resumed our voyage southward.

We eventually came across a large island to our left, which we judged to be about ten miles in length and five miles in breadth, but decided that this was not the land we sought, this was not the new found land, just another large island and not worth our time to explore at this time, Arn just marked it upon his chart, rolled them up again in their sealskin coverings and pointed southwards. We continued on for another ten leagues distance, slowly beginning to realise we had entered a huge strait, with numerous small icebergs still present despite the season having progressed into late spring. They filled the entire waterway, making navigation potentially dangerous and necessitating a good lookout at all times. It also precluded any thought of night-time sailing, with the very early mornings also being somewhat hazardous, due to the thick enveloping fog, which luckily quickly burnt off with the rising of the sun. The strait was quite possibly five leagues' wide width, according to Arn's reckoning. The mainland lay to our right; with the land we could now see on our left we felt sure was a truly large island. Arn was further convinced that this land was indeed the same land that we sought,

Leif also thought this was most likely our new found land, a land that we had almost reached last autumn, only to have Loki as usual play one of his tricks by sending those accursed winds and currents that had driven us North West ward, and at the same time had split our mast and forced us ashore for the winter.

Arn bade our helmsman bear to the right and hug the coast, to give us the opportunity to seek out a suitable landing place. Although we had only come about a hundred leagues from our winter camp, it had been decided by Arn and the others that we had now at last done enough. It was now midsummer, we had spent too much time exploring up and down the coast, we had entered creeks and rivers and gone ashore to explore all we thought that were of interest, we had spent so much time doing this that summer had now all but escaped us, winter was not the season for exploration, we knew that the time had now come when we must return home to Norway. Perhaps it would be prudent to return via Iceland, and let the authorities know of our discoveries; we owed it to the people there to let them know of these new lands that lay only a few hundred leagues away from their doorstep, they can do as they wish with the information we give them.

We decided that we would find somewhere to stay anchored for a couple of days, and then after resting we would turn northwards again back up through the strait. After a while we indeed found a suitable place to layover for a while, entering into a large bay where we lay close in to the beach, the water being quite shallow here with algae covered pebbles being clearly visible below us. We secured the boat at the prow with a rope attached to a mooring stake driven hard into the shale and pebble beach, our stone anchor remained in its storage space we wanted to be able to leave the beach quickly if Skraelings suddenly appeared.

Orn and myself along with Guilli had asked to go ashore before our return voyage we made the pretence that it was to be our final hunting trip before returning north wards once more. In reality it was to be free of work for a few hours, I expect Arn saw through our plan but had just shrugged his shoulders saying to keep our eyes open and be careful. We had enjoyed a winter of comparative idleness; a full day's work now become hard to get used to once more, and we had little free time to ourselves for several months now. The three of us waded ashore and walked inland a mile or so and entered a more densely wooded area where we found an animal track which we followed for a short distance which finally brought us into a small clearing. There was something moving in the undergrowth on the other side of the clearing which turned out to be a small deer, for some reason it seemed not to realise we were there, there was a slight breeze coming towards us across the clearing, strong enough to ruffle my hair and to stop the deer catching our scent. Orn notched an arrow to his bow and brought the deer down with a single shot, by his own admission it was a lucky shot as he had not had a completely clear view of the animal. We tallied awhile longer in the forest but in truth in the few hours we were ashore we did not see any more game, the forest path like clearing itself had numerous pad marks left by wolves in the soft ground which probably explained all. We gutted then deer there and then being sure to keep the offal and then shouldered the deer between two of us, having just tied its legs together and putting an ash pole between them to ease carrying it back to the ship. As we walked back along the forest path the same way that we had entered it, Guilli turned towards Orm and myself saying that he that he had the distinct feeling that we were being watched, but by wolf or man he did not know, he said it was just a feeling that he had, and he couldn't shake it. There certainly seemed also to be a lot of evidence supporting the fact there were many wolves in the area. Maybe they were scaring the game away, we surmised, so we did not dally long, returning early afternoon to the vessel without further incident.

On our return I found that Arn had spent most of the day poring over his charts; modifying them with the latest information that we had gleaned since leaving the winter camp. That evening he called us altogether and announced that at first light we would turn northward once more for the return trip. He said he did not want to venture further down the strait, not knowing what the wind and current would be like, for eventually we would have to return back up the strait, and he did not wish for us to have to row all the way and sap our strength with such a long way to go before we would return to home waters.

He said he was also greatly concerned about our new mast and thought that the sail itself would perhaps not stand up to many heavy winds. He further reasoned that he thought the island opposite our present anchorage here on the mainland could indeed prove to be immense, and as such would be too great a distance for us to circumnavigate in the time left to us. We must he said, be back in Iceland by late autumn at the latest, and it was therefore his decision that we would start back at dawn. He estimated that we had a voyage of maybe two hundred and fifty leagues of open sea to cross. We knew land would lay to our west, but it would be too far away even to contemplate putting in to replenish the contents of our water casks. He said he would not risk totally losing the vessel on an unexplored coast; we had already been down that path. We had achieved so much; he would not throw it all away along with our lives on what may turn out to be a fruitless exploration. Once we had sailed past the general vicinity of our winter camp site, there would be no turning back, it would be crucial that we make the voyage back to Iceland in one long haul, or perish in the attempt, this land here is misleading, the lands got everything we need for now, but to spend another winter here could well prove our undoing and see us all to the afterlife. We must leave it now or resign ourselves for staying here for eternity; we cannot winter over again with most of our supplies gone, what's left up at the palisade will not help us through another winter. We were lucky not to be found last winter by the Skraelings, we may not be so lucky next time, once they find us I think that they will not leave us alone. They will most likely think of as invaders in their lands and I have this feeling that they will not rest until they see us all dead or gone from their lands. I looked back at the bay we had left behind us, Arn had marked it on his charts as being the bay of wolves, after we had told him of our thoughts as to why there seemed a lack of game there. He had listened seriously to Guilli when he repeated again that he thought that we had been observed after we had killed the deer.

All Arn said was

'It's as well that we are away from this place then as soon as possible'

We set sail the next morning as soon as it was light and made our way out into mid channel and started our voyage back up the ice strewn strain channel and out into the open sea, then turning north east for what we hoped would be an easy run up into Reykjavík, Arn said we would be back on the coast of Iceland within a couple of weeks or so if we had fair winds and currents. Never with Arn was it a case of him saying we might have problems finding our way, he was always so sure of his ability to navigate anywhere and make that distant landfall and it was uncanny at times. I think the only thing now that played on his mind was us not having enough fresh water and supplies to last the voyage and I know he fretted continually over the state of our new mast, if it were to break then the ship and ourselves were doomed.

As time went on and I became to know Arn and him me, he seemed to want to take me more and more into his confidence, I think the burden of command weight heavily on his shoulders at times and he wanted to share some of the decisions that had to be made, or at least run his idea's past someone else before he implemented them. We sat huddled in the stern of the ship one evening looking up at the star strewn sky and checking our bearing in relation to the great pole star.

Arn turned to me and said

'You know Olaf I did think that we might have made a profit out of this voyage of discovery of ours, don't get me wrong that's all it was ever really have meant to be but one's got to be realistic as well, the people back in Iceland are going to listen to our tales with interest, but no one is going to follow in our footsteps. It's too great a risk for people to up roots from what they have and know, leaving everything behind them and sail over to this new land and start to make a life there for themselves. When they hear we lost men out there to hostile Skraelings and that the winters are just as severe as our own, it's going to be years before they come to these lands, they will also remember about the colonists who went to the Greenland and have never been heard of again, they were never resupplied and the same thing would happen to people here trying to hack out an existence on the new found land or on the mainland itself. They would also have to contend with attacks from the Skraelings, they are a savage race and once they knew that our people had come to their land to stay indefinitely they perhaps would never leave them in peace, the resources here are good but not without limit, they would not be willing to share them with our people indefinitely and why should they? It's their land after all. Moreover how many Skraelings live in these lands? Our people could simply be overwhelmed in an unexpected attack. More exploration of these lands is necessary before our people can come here to live in any numbers'

'I will tell the authorities of our exploration on the coast, but I will not make an issue of it and ask them to fund another expedition. This trip has not ruined me financially but it has cost me dearly, especially as I will now need to get the boat repaired, a new mast and sail for sure so I need to organise a few good cargos for us to transport when we arrive back home, and for us to make some quick money. We may even have to go raiding again for a while if those cargos can't be found quickly. We will find that old drunkard Bjarni when we get back to Norway, last I heard of him he was still up to his old tricks and was raiding down as far as the south coast of Wessex and even up the creeks and rivers into the land of the Franks, if needs be and depending on what Bjarni has to say, we can do the same for a while'

Once we had cleared the channel, we set sail northeast-ward with some trepidation, Arn wanted us to sail directly for Iceland, but most of the men were alarmed at the great distance involved, Arn soon silenced them by saying there was no alternative, our ship was sound and we had provisioned it as best we could, we can make it back to Iceland and he finally closed the matter by saying he knew exactly our position in relation to the green land.

This probably was the main thing that the men wanted to know at this moment in time; if they had faith in Arn's navigation then they would cause no further problem in this direction. Arn said he would show us the southern tip of the green land in about two hundred leagues distance. From there it was another two and fifty leagues back to Iceland, if the worse came to the worse we could put into a Fjord on the green land for fresh water, but he said he really wanted to waste no time in exploring that land. It was going to be a difficult journey, but we had made it across the western ocean without it being to arduous not even knowing where our destination lay, so surely we could return the same way and make landfall on the coast of Iceland with no problems. We would collect rain water to top up our barrels of water and put our long lines out to catch fish to supplement the dried fish and seal meat we had processed during the summer months, we would survive.

As it was when we sighted the tip of the green land the weather turned on us and we thought it prudent to seek the shelter of the land, so we sailed parallel to the coast for about sixty leagues coming up to an island that looked as if it had deep shelving beaches. We anchored in as close as we dare and had no choice but to take all that the storm threw at us, it buffeted us with high winds and the ship wallowed like a sow in mire and we were soaked to the skin by the cold stinging rain. When the storm eventually exhausted itself we sent men ashore to look for fresh water. We found the fresh water we sought without a problem but there was nothing else here it was truly a desolate unforgiving coast line. We fished and repaired our clothes and made minor repairs to the boat, finding enough drift wood to light a fire which we then fed with anything we thought would burn and managed to dry our damp and mouldy clothes but there was precious little wood to be found on the beach and nothing further inland. We cooked some hot food which raised the men's morale and the talk turned to the next leg of our voyage to Iceland, everyone was hoping for a short stay there before committing to the final leg of our voyage back home to Norway. The men were glad for a respite from the vigour's of being out on the open ocean... Arn allowed us all sometime ashore to stretch our legs and to explore the island, the mood of the crew now changed and they were back to their normal optimistic selves, especially as their confidence in Arn as a navigator, if indeed it had ever really wavered, had been restored. He had brought us to the coast of the green land just as he said he would, it even being in the time scale that Arn had said it would be. We knew that we were almost back to civilisation, after all as Snorri, who hailed from Iceland had told us often, that from the high ground near his home in western Iceland on a very clear day you could see the distant peaks of Greenland. We left our welcome refuge and sailed due east for Reykjavik, veering to the north east after about five- or six-days sail. The following day we saw high above us birds screeching and calling to each other. Land was near, Arn had proved to us all again what an able navigator he was. Most of the crew thought he had some divine gift, few realised that when he was seen holding his talisman up by its leather throng that it was this object that was continually pointing the way northward, and combined with Arn's knowledge of the western ocean and just importantly him knowing more or less where our ship lay that was showing him the way home. It was not only his talisman that helped him, I knew that Arn looked at the size of the waves and the colour of the sea, the presence or absence of seabirds above us and in what direction they flew, even taking into consideration whether or not there was seaweed floating in the current, all of these things taken together meant something to him.

The next day laying low on the horizon we saw Iceland; most of us had been thinking that we would never see its shores again. We came through a throng of small fishing vessels, most not giving us a second glance. When we were up to one of the piers and started to tie the boat up we began to attract some more serious stares. I was on the dock, tying the vessel up astern and as I looked from the crowd that had now gathered, back to our boat things must have appeared strange to them. The mast looked odd now in the cold light of day, the sail was patched like a quilt and all the rigging was frayed and as our men came under the scrutiny of the onlookers on the dock we must have appeared to them to be in a sad and sorry state. Our clothes were torn and in tatters, our hair and beards were un shorn and matted we must have looked like warriors down on their luck, which perhaps was not too far from the truth.

Presently some port officials came down and Arn disappeared into the town with them, leaving to my bewilderment myself in charge of the boat. The people on the dock were now anxious to hear our story, I thought no harm in telling them where we had been, that we had voyaged beyond the western horizon to a distant land and seen all kind of new and mysterious things and how we had fought a strange and savage people that knew no metal and used only stone axes and tipped their arrows with arrow heads made of flint. They even painted and tattooed their entire bodies, and had proved to us what formidable fighters they were in mortal combat. I think that most of the people were somewhat sceptical of the truth of our stories, not that we cared either way if they believed us or not.

We stayed in Iceland for several weeks, Arn had his boat dragged ashore and several things repaired, but our mast that Guilli had so painstaking made was deemed to be sound and so it stayed in its block, with Guilli beaming with pride when the local ship wrights told him he had done an amazing job with so little tools. We all when ashore and bought new clothes and sea boots, we trimmed our hair and beards. We saw to our weapons and mail shirts and then disappeared into the taverns of the town looking for women and strong drink. Myself and Leif along with Guilli entering the tavern behind the fish warehouse and for a while all the locals thought we had taken up permanent residence there. Arn joined us a few days later, saying the response from the authorities on our discovery

121

of land across the western ocean was much as he expected, they had listened politely and asked numerous questions even asking for some charts of the coast line we had explored. However as Arn had originally thought that in most likelihood would be an end to it, as he had told me a few months earlier he would not labour the point and didn't ask for funds to mount another expedition, so he had just thanked them and returned to the ship and thence up to this tavern to rejoin Guilli and myself. A few weeks later, our boat repaired and once more back in the water we set sail back to Norway and home. Arn as usual had managed to pick up a small cargo of salted fish in barrels and three or four people who were willing to pay for the passage back to Norway.

Chapter Eleven

After our return home to Norway, it was not long before Arn realised that he desperately needed money to be able to resume the way of life that he had followed before he went on his voyage of exploration, he knew the ship could still do with some more work on it, perhaps it really needed replacing, there were palms to grease as he tried to re-establish contracts with his old trading partners, maybe he thought that it would even be a good idea to rent or buy a ware house somewhere or other.

He took me into his confidence one evening and we spoke candidly about what we thought most likely lay in the future for the pair of us and for the crew, he stated the obvious concerning the boat. We both knew that it would need replacement sooner rather than later, and he didn't really need to remind me the voyage we had undertaken across the great western ocean had showed hardly any profit all. We came back with our lives and tall tales that some people would not believe were true and some furs and walrus tusk and that was about all. The gold and silver we sought had evaded us; any money that we had left was given to the crew. Olaf I am going to find it hard if not impossible to pay for the up keep of the boat and the men still have not been paid in full, they should be paid for the hardships they endured during the last couple of winters, they never complained and did everything that I asked off them and more besides. Without a boat I have nothing Olaf I cannot go and work on someone's else boat at my age and for us to be able to return to our previous way of life we need money and quickly, I must pay the men, some have families and it must have been hard for them, they were loyal to me and now I must repay that loyalty. I cannot see any other way around this problem other than to go raiding one more time if I can persuade the men to come with me. Just one successful raid along the coastline of Francia is all I ask for. A few months more and all will be back to normal and by the end of the year we will have all the money we need or we will all be lying dead in the bottom of the boat with Frank arrows through our mail and it won't matter either way then.

Bjarni's name came up in our conversation, we had raided with him once before but nobody seemed to know where he was now or when he would return. We felt we could not justify a long wait, not even being completely sure he would return to this part of Norway at all and for that matter the old rascals luck could have run out up some Frankish river and that he had already been dead for some months or years. Those Frankish ports were sometimes well protected and if you raided the wrong one without sufficient forward planning you could well find the tables turned upon you, with all the jokes apart the Franks were no easy foe to overcome, armed with sword and shield they were a force to be reckoned with, which is why these men were so prized as mercenaries..

However we had been told about a man called Steinvidr who like Bjarni also raided along the coast of Francia, Bjarni occasionally taking his ship and crew on joint raids with this man so we thought that we would have nothing to lose by speaking with the man, reasoning that if Bjarni trusted him then that would go a long way in helping us to commit ourselves to going on a raid with him, trust was everything on these joint raids.

We thought that we could set up an initial meeting with the man and sound him out, and indeed to show him see what manner of men that we were, trust goes both ways and he would as yet not have heard about us or any of the things that we had accomplished, Arn liked to keep things quiet and not draw undue attention to himself or his boat. We needed this meeting to go well Arn knew full well that we needed this man's help, we could not successfully hope to accomplish a raid on the coast of Francia on our own and to contemplate raiding up the creeks and inlets there with no prior knowledge of the lay of the land and the general situation down there would be reckless to say the least if not verging on suicide

We made a few inquiries and found that Steinvidr had his boat docked in a port further to the south so we sent a message to him asking for a meeting, we felt no harm in telling his that we were friends of Bjarni and wanted to discuss going on a raid with him, he could agree to a meeting or just ignore us we had nothing to lose by meeting with him but everything to gain

We sailed down to the fjord to where the port lay nestled under a huge overhanging rock outcrop but a short distance from the entrance to the fjord, well protected from the oceans ravages during the winter months, we had all been here several times before in previous years. Apparently Steinvidr used it as his base when not raiding and was well known in the small town, his presence from time to time probably helping towards the town's prosperity. We docked without incident a couple of days later sending word of our arrival into the town, knowing news travelled fast in these small ports and that news of our arrival we knew would not be long in reaching Steinvidr's ears if it had not done so already. You don't engage in the line of work that Steinvidr followed without keeping your ear to the ground and paying people to keep you abreast of information, your safety and indeed your life could depend upon it.

We thought a good a place as any to try and contact Steinvidr would be at the end of the quay where there was a tavern attached to a warehouse, Arn said he remembered the place from previous visits to the port, so with this objective in mind I accompanied Arn to the tavern where we could await his arrival and then hopefully we could discuss the possibility of joining him on one of the raids that he now had such good a reputation for making

We waited outside the tavern for him to show and sure enough presently we saw a wiry little man approaching accompanied by two other heavily armed men with shields across their backs and axe and sword at their belts. The trio stopping from time to time to speak with some of the other people on the quay, they seemed to know everyone present and acted as if they owned the dock and its adjacent warehouses.

When he saw us and realised that we were most likely the people that he had come to see he said something to his two companions provoking a short laugh from this gruff pair, they were most likely his body guards and Steinvidr could not have picked a better pair for the job I though, a right pair of evil looking bastards. They turned in our direction and started to cross the short distance between us, it now being clear we were now the centre of Steinvidr's attention. He scowled at a group of children nearby who scuttled away like a plague of cockroaches suddenly disturbed raiding a flour barrel and disappeared down into a nearby alleyway, probably looking for easier pickings and having more sense than to cross this cantankerous old man. He swore at some poor unfortunate who had managed to get in his way, one of his body guards cuffing the man around the ear for good measure which sent him on his way without further ado.

Surprisingly when Steinvidr approached us his weather beaten and heavily lined face broke out into a broad smile showing gaps in his black and broken teeth. His mottled skin had the constituency and colour of a pickled walnut. A scar ran from his forehead terminating at his chin, probably a slash from a sword and he was probably lucky not to have lost the eye.

I could tell that he was the warrior of renown that our informant had tried to describe to us, and now I could understand how Bjarni would be willing to accompany such a man as this on raids into unknown and dangerous territory, he seemed to exhibit that strength of character that such men have and to give of an absolute air of confidence which all fighting men wanted to see in their chosen leader.

He wore a heavy leather jerking with metal rings sewed onto it which would at least have helped prevent a blow from a sword causing too much damage and over this he wore the same sleeveless sheepskin jacket that his two men wore. The attitude of his two men now seemed to have taken on a more relaxed way, seemingly already having apprised the pair of us and come to the conclusion we were no threat to their master. He held his hand out to Arn, I suppose he thought that I was Arn's bodyguard and only made a cursory nod in my direction.

He said he had been expecting the pair of us, not even asking who we were just seemingly to know that we were the two men he had been told about by our messenger.

He told us to follow him, we were half expecting him to take us into the tavern a few hundred feet away but he said he had a house nearby and it would be away from prying eyes and ears and we could discuss our plans in private without half the dock knowing our business within the hour. He already seemingly having made his mind up about us already, perhaps Bjarni had mentioned to him previously that it was Arn's crew who has accompanied him when he had raided that Scottish monastery a few years back.

As we walked with him he told us that this was his home port and that he controlled most of the dock side, there's a lot of thieving on the other quays, but not on mine I won't tolerate it.

I barely suppressed a smile, here was this man, most likely the biggest thief in all of southwest Norway saying that he does not tolerate thievery on the dock and I could see from the look on his face that he was being serious..

I looked at the man as we walked, he had that lean hungry look of expectation of things and adventures to come he walked with a confidence that was half swagger and half seaman's roll not quite sure if the land under his feet was going to give way and start to move like the pitch and roll of a ship's deck. I had also seen that same look in Bjarni's eyes when I had briefly been with him on the whale road. I could see that they were both cast from the same mould, and how they had been drawn to this life as a bee is drawn to the honey pot, they could not help themselves or avoid it, no more than they could stop breathing, it was their fate, they were doing what men of the northlands were born to do. It made me think that this grizzly old man, a man now of almost sixty years was of the same stock as Bjarni and all the others that I had encountered along the way, it made me warm towards him even more and in a strange way to be proud to be in their company even thou they were in reality thieves and cut throats and most likely worse. Leaving my home and my father behind me to fish their Fjord day after day was the best decision that I ever could have made it was giving me the opportunity now to understand myself, the race of people who I was descended from and help me perhaps to see clearly and to follow more easily the path that Odin had so obviously laid out for me, and I thanked them all for it, but at times in truth I did not always like what I saw and was forced to do on occasion.

We entered Steinvidr 's house, which in reality was not much more than a warehouse, I doubt if he spent hardly any time here at all, but it boasted a table and chairs with a few sleeping cots against the wall. We sat around the table, one of his thrall's silently and unbidden appeared from out the back carrying ale and mead.

Arn and I took to the man immediately, he was strait forward and it was obvious to all and sundry that he knew his business, we were truthful and told him we were only looking to join him for the one raiding party, perhaps down to Francia the land of the Franks, anywhere where there was money to be made and where we had a slight chance of coming back home again relatively unscathed. He laughed and said

'It could well be your only raid with me if things go wrong'

The implication off these words not being lost on us as were their intention and it was to be the only warning he ever gave to us of the dangers off what to expect down there on the coast of Francia.

We told him where we had been the last couple of years, he listened intently seeming impressed with our stories and concluding that perhaps we should count ourselves lucky to have returned at all. He seemed more than satisfied with us and said that he remembered us going with Bjarni to raid the monastery and its land in Scotland a few years back. It was enough we had a partner and a chance to make some money and possible be alive at the end of it all to spend it.

Chapter Twelve

We set sail from Norway following in Steinvidr's wake sailing southward down through the north sea and then westward into the channel that separated the south coast of Wessex from the coast of Francia.

Steinvidr said he knew or thought he knew of a part of the coast line that was not patrolled by more than one or two of their boats. He further suspected the few rivers along that stretch of coastline would not be well protected if at all and he was equally sure there would be no chains across these smaller rivers. Chains across rivers were about the worse nightmare scenario one could ever envisage, that most likely would end in the capture of your boat and all your crew killed, it would leave your boat trapped and vulnerable to attack from the riverbanks and you unable able to proceed further and an even worse scenario would be if another boat full of warriors had unknowingly followed you up river, so that you were completely trapped not even able to get back to the open ocean.

Notwithstanding all the risks it was still these small towns and villages up the creeks and rivers that attracted us, we knew them to be profitable and mostly unprotected except for the port captain and a handful of his underpaid soldiers. Steinvidr said that he knew there were several islands up one of these rivers which had at least one busy port and a town constructed behind the port and as such he thought there should have much wealth attached to it, gold, hack silver and amber for sure to pay the ships captains who traded with the towns people, there would be furs and any other trade goods in the ware houses most likely just here for the taking and at this time of the year there may be slaves as well. There would also be the opportunity to take slaves from the local population, Frankish women brought high prices in the markets back home and were even more valuable when traded down the rivers through the land of the Rus and then across the black sea into the Byzantine city of Miklagard. It was well know that the local caliph down there preferred white skinned women in their harems. We had even heard it rumoured that if one was really down on one's luck maybe having been outlawed from your homeland for some transgression real or imaged it was possible to hire out to these people as mercenaries, the caliph's there trusting men from the north lands and Wessex more than their own guard's.

So all in all we considered that this venture was well worth the risk, just to go and have a look was worth it, and then maybe to return the following year, better organised and with more men and boats if we needed to.

We arrived down on the coast of Francia without incident apart from a slight encounter with some raiders out of Frisia who by chance had spotted us and gave chase, but as they got closer they realised that we were a raiding party like themselves and thought better of coming any closer and slowly they slipped behind us into our wake leaving us once more alone on the open ocean.

We arrived at the mouth of the first river with the intention of raiding up this inlet which would lead us to our first objective which was the two islands mid river and the port and city built there, if sacking this city and its port brought enough riches we would not have to push our luck and raid anywhere else on this coast line, at least not on this voyage.

We rowed up the river not really attracting any un due attention with Arn remarking that he thought that was odd in itself, it all seemed a bit too easy, we kept our voices low just in case people along the river banks heard us speaking Norse and wondered why two Norse vessels were coming up river alone, usually you would have to pay a tariff to the port captain to enter these rivers but we had not seen any vessels and no one had bothered to come out and meet us, their incompetence was our gain as we had initially been prepared for a fight at the mouth of the river as we tried to come upstream which would have betrayed our presence sooner than we would have liked. Another bonus was the fact that as yet we had not seen any evidence of chains across the river.

We saw a few dwellings along the river bank with a cow or two tethered nearby and we could hear the sound of children laughing, all seemed as it should be. There was a herd of goats grazing down by the water's edge seemingly not worried by our presence but of the goat herder himself there was no sign.

After an hour or less we arrived at the first of the islands, there were in any case only two of any size, there were a few much smaller ones, but these were hardly worth our time to investigate. We presently came up to a quite unremarkable small port that was nestled on the western tip of the larger of the islands; it was just a collection of huts with the obligatory wooden quay. It was a bleak place; no trees were in evidence on the island, most likely if there ever had been any they had long since been cut down for firewood. There was not much here on the distant river banks, the channel either side of the islands seemed to be quite wide but there was nothing on these banks for several hundred yards, nothing but waterlogged land with a mist still hanging over it which would have to wait until the sun rose to disperse it probably not too healthy a place to live I thought..

There were several beached and anchored boats lying hither and thither with apparently no thought of organisation. There was a small cargo boat alongside the rickety quay, she looked like a sturdy vessel suitable for sailing from port to port close in to shore, but not built for heavy seas there were also a few small river craft alongside the quay it looked like the cargo boat was discharging her goods into them. There was a number of small fishing boats pulled up onto the beach for repairs with men repairing nets strung out to dry on poles alongside the beaches

It was a pitiful place but it served its purpose, I along with some of the other men were now beginning to wonder how much longer it would be before we attracted some serious attention as it hardly seemed the kind of port two large sea going vessels would want to dock in especially unannounced and I was beginning to think that maybe we had made a grave error venturing up this river and putting ourselves at risk, and most likely for little if any reward by the look of the town behind the port.

We anchored off the beach of the larger island; people were now beginning to show a great deal of interest in our two vessels. There were some armed men on horseback riding down towards the beach, most likely the port captain having at long last been roused and come to collect his long overdue tariff. We were here to raid and it almost seemed that it was the complete opposite that we had come for peaceful trade. Steinvidr stirred us all shouting across to Arn to get his men ready and do what we had come to this place for. Men slipped over the side of the two boats into the shallow water and started wading ashore, not really expecting any resistance. The port captain and his men were slow to react not quite comprehending the serious of events that were beginning to unfold.

Once ashore the inevitable happened, our men once unleashed were like a pack of wild dogs. It sickened me to see how they were behaving, but it was pointless to try and intervene. Steinvidr, so hardened to this kind of thing would not condemn it, Arn powerless and unwilling to say anything, he was nobody's fool and he knew all along that it would be like this, he had been on the whale road himself for years before he took to peace full trading. This was the way it was and the way perhaps it should be for men of the north lands. Once our men were in the town behind the port the massacre began people were killed for no reason, they had nothing to give us and had nowhere to run; many were slaves and offered no resistance. We could have taken them as prisoners, but had I not just before we waded ashore uttered out of my own mouth to our men the command that we were not to overburden ourselves with prisoners and slaves. I had no idea this raid was going to unfold like this, I should have known it would always be like this thou, but I suppose deep down I never really did could come to grips with the notion of all this wanton killing, I had been on revenge raids many times before and had also attacked monasteries feeling no remorse, I had participated in killing scores of the white Christ devils who were not even worthy of being called men, but somehow that was different in my eyes, the bulk of our men had understood my orders regarding the taking of slaves and there had been no disagreements or mutterings within our ranks as they knew that the order had really come from Arn and Steinvidr. The bulk of them anyway were just interested in the gold, silver and jewels. There was always the same problem when taking prisoners as well as slaves, they had to be guarded and looked after, and utilising men for guarding prisoners was never popular with anyone especially when there was still plunder to be taken. There was always the risk that the prisoners would turn on the

137

guard detail once they realised they had nothing to lose. With that in mind most of our men thought it was easier just to kill these people and not bother taking prisoners and content themselves to taking slaves when the fighting was over and the local population subdued.

I was no coward and I have always considered myself as being a true man of the north lands and I have never had any qualms about killing white Christ priests to prevent them poisoning the minds of our people with their lies and to stop their greed and influence spreading, to be asked to kill in battle and to even kill other men of the northlands then you would hear no objection from me, but this senseless murder and waste of innocents I always had problems coming to terms with.

Towards the end men started returning to their ships, I looked from the shore line across at Steinvidr's ship, it looked as if they had taken twenty slaves or so onboard, indeed it looked like the captives could well be white Christ priests as they wore the brown habits that we had come to associate with such creatures, all of a sudden there was a great deal of commotion and shouting and some of Steinvidr's men for reasons unknown to us at this distance suddenly attacked the group of men who had huddled together as if that would offer them some protection, and our men literally hacked them to pieces with their axes in front of our eyes and cast their bodies into the river.

We went from one house to another, searching for booty and raping and killing as we went. All who stood up to us we hacked to pieces, drowning many in the nearby river and leaving their bodies in the water to be tossed this way as the water lapped the river bank, bodies becoming bloated and swollen to twice their normal size in the sun until their bellies burst and spilled their intestines out into river only to be eaten by the towns dogs who knew that they had masters no more and had already formed into scavenging packs.

We continued killing and looting with some of the citizens trying to surrender to us without a fight, many of these were unable or unwilling to give us what we wanted so we stabbed and hacked or burnt them to death and our men drown a great many of them in the surrounding waters.

They were like a fox in a hen house not knowing when enough was enough and always wanting more.

It was time to go we had sacked this island and the neighbouring one of its wealth, we found hack silver and gold maybe not as much as we would have liked but it was enough for us to have all become wealthy men. We found warehouses full of furs and all manner of trade items, amber in abundance with ivory and bone waiting to be worked. We had taken about twenty women prisoners, all were good looking strong and healthy and we would take them back to Norway to decide where we could sell them for the best profit, some might be lucky and be bought by local men at home to be taken as wives and would then live a good life amongst our people and eventually no longer be thought of as slaves.

We loaded all of our plunder and boarded our boats positioning ourselves mid river, ready for the attempt to sail downstream, it was not that tidal this far up the river but at least the river was flowing towards the sea and helped as we rowed hard back up the short distance to the river mouth our sail not helping us greatly as this section of the river seemed all but devoid of any breeze. It had all been so easy we were ever fearful that we would come to an abrupt stop pulled up by a chain across the river or we would meet with a couple of boatful of armed warriors coming up river having being sent to investigate reports of problems on the island, but nothing like this transpired, it had all been so quick there was no time for our presence to have been reported and we know the ports captain and his men could not have made such a report as they now lay dead at the bottom of the river with most of the other towns folk. Even as we neared the river's mouth we were fretful that we could well find our exit blockaded and our lives forfeit. However there were no other vessels in sight apart from a few fishing boats a long way out in the distance, and even if they saw us emerging from the river they would most likely not think anything was amiss

As we came to the mouth of the river and entered the ocean once more for our voyage home we encountered bad weather, we saw rain showers on the distant horizon that looked like pillars of black granite descending from the sky to the sea, then they were gone seemingly dispersed by the wind or just emptying their contents on to the surface of the sea and flattening it and presenting a false like calm.

Then violent storms sprung up from these clear skies which one moment had been a calm flat blue sea with hardly a trace of a breeze and then the next minute gale force winds were whipping at our sails and threatening to tear our masts from their very blocks. We found our ships beginning to be separated by this tremendous storm, the lighting flashed and the sound of thunder was so loud you could not hear the man standing next to you shouting into your ear. It was terrifying, men were cowering in the bottom of the boats calling out to their god's to protect them, but it was to no avail Thor welded his battle axe time and time again at imaginary foes or otherwise as he drove his chariot ever westward across a darkening sky causing the lighting to crackle as it sought its earth mate and salvation by descending to the ocean below causing the water to hiss and boil. Thor as usual showed no mercy towards Tanngrisni and Tanngnost as he urged them ever onwards with his whip causing the sound of thunder to intensify until one's ears could hardly bear it. Steinvidr brought his boat as close as he dared to Arn's and shouted across to him that he had decided that our two long ships must now go Northeast ward and then along the coast of Frisia turning eventually northward and up to Norway. We had two ships full of plunder and a few slaves, we were not to risk losing everything, including our lives by raiding up any more creeks or rivers the weather had turned against us and the coast and waters of the Franks would not be safe for us for many years to come. We knew that some of the people that we had just murdered were probably second or third generation men of the north living in land of the Franks, we might now even find ourselves outlawed because of the deeds we have committed this day and Arn would then presently find himself permanently back on the whale road with Steinvidr. After all we had committed outrage upon outrage during our time upon this river and the things we had done on that island in the port and its town would be seen as being nothing short of pure evil

For now thou we had money, more than enough to give us what we wanted for years to come, we had slaves and other items to trade. We must now go our separate ways, for Steinvidr to continue the only life he knew on the whale road, but it was time now for Arn to return to his peace full trading or to undertake further voyages of exploration

Steinvidr's plan made sense and Arn was in agreement with him and didn't try to argue with his decision, they all saw the sense of it and so we set sail in a north east direction in the general direction of home, we all felt a great deal more secure when we turned and looked in our wake and saw that there were no ships trailing us.

Arn turned to me saying

'Let us leave this land of the Franks and go home, they can take their bad luck with them to their graves and those that still live can hope that they never come across men from the northlands again'

When we returned home again now having been absent for a long time and seen a great many things I found life to be even more strange and difficult to adjust to. I know a lot of the other men were having the same problems as me. Life here in the villages and fjords had continued much the same as before I had left, everything seemed the same, it's slow pace of life being one of the very reasons that I had wanted to leave in the first place, but at least I could console myself in the knowledge that I had seen more adventure in the last couple of years than others perhaps would have in an entire lifetime. My father was still in good health and continued his fishing out on the fjord, thou he had employed a local man to help him with the boat. I habitually stayed at his house for the period of time I was to be in port, but my father never asked me once if I was prepared to join him on his vessel fishing out in the fjord, only saying to me

'I suppose you will be remaining working with Arn, thou even that may seem a bit boring for you now after all these adventures you have had the last few years. I hear he has already organised a few local voyages, his boat was badly missed upon the coast all that time you were away'

The question in my opinion didn't really need an answer; he already must have realised that I would continue sailing with Arn. So I returned onboard Arn's vessel and we carried on much the same as before we had left for our voyage across the western ocean. We all stayed together as a crew for a number of years, spending our time sailing from one port to the other along the Norwegian coast and occasionally down to Denmark, thou that was always a risky voyage. The Jarl's down there were still having problems with their renegades, and you never quite knew when one of their long boats, packed with warriors dressed in mail and spoiling for a fight would come silently out of the mist with grappling hooks and come along side your vessel and before you knew it they would be pouring over the side of your vessel like honey dripping down the sides of a pot with axe in hand.

Then at the end of one voyage Ranald announced he was giving the sea up, he surprised us all he had turned out well, and had been with us a number of years now, he was heavily muscled now and had acquired a few tattoos along the way and looked just like any other man of the north now. He was a good man to have on a row bench and was a good a man with a bow as you could hope to have. In a tight spot, in a real bad situation he was able to keep his head and still hit what he was aiming at and we knew we would miss him. What we probably wouldn't miss was having to carry him back to the ship dead drunk when we were in port, in that direction he had become as bad as Leif. He did periodically thou do the odd trip here and there for us when Arn was short-handed. Gurt had left us the very day we had returned from Iceland and had not accompanied us on our raid with Steinvidr down into the land of the Franks, he was getting on in years now and was anxious to see his family and farm again, and nothing we could say would persuade him to return to the sea going life again, enough is enough we often heard him say. He had returned to his farm and his family, not much richer than when he left, but he had his one last adventure and settled down with his two sons to working his farm, which prospered from their hard work, more than the influx of the money he had originally sought. He never left his farm again, other to come down to the village and look up old friends. He was a regular visitor to my father's house when I was in port, where we never tired of telling each other the same stories over and over again, whilst we consumed our ale. He lived to a good old age, dying peacefully in his bed a couple of years later, his wife and two sons and their tribe of numerous wild children in attendance. Gradually the rest of the crew began to drift away, just a natural occurrence of people's fortunes changing or just wanting something else out of life. Arn was naturally disappointed, but as he said to me one day, no one man owns a ship's crew, we are peaceful traders, we are not on the whale road any more where I would ask all my crew to swear an oath of allegiance to me, they are all free to do as they wish. Leif left the ship after a few more years. He married a buxom widow woman from the next village up the coast who ran a drinking establishment. Later to my utter amazement my friend Bjorn purchased a farm, married a local woman and hung up his axe and shield. The following year Jarl and his brother Geirr were also to leave the vessel, to take over the family farm I heard. Eventually the only members of the originally crew was Arn and myself, Arn having by now made me sailing master, a great honour and I know my father was immensely proud of me that night we sat in companionable conversation in front of a roaring fire, drinking mulled ale, as I told him of my promotion, and my hopes and aspirations for my future life onboard Arn's vessel. We seemed to get along better now after the death of my grandfather than we had previously ever had.

Arn and I had now out of necessity recruited more men to crew the boat without effort, after all Arn and his boat had a good, well-earned reputation on the coast, and as far away as Iceland, so it had not been a problem. One day Arn came around to my house, it was about mid-morning my father was not there, he was still out in the fjord with his hired man 'fishing. 'Olaf I want to ask your advice on a couple of matters,' he said

'What would you say if I told you that I have arranged to purchase another vessel, our present one has served us well, it's still got that mast from the tree we felled in those western lands that we discovered, but I think it will not stand up to the voyage I am contemplating.'

Here it comes I thought, I had been expecting this conversation for some time now, he continued unabated saying that he was thinking of buying a new vessel from old Sveinn's son 'You know the man I think, a good ship builder, he builds and buys ships up at Bjorgvin, I have already seen the boat, she is named "Curlew" a good name, which I think we will keep. She is a magnificent looking sea going boat, sturdy but a bit broad in the beam just the way I like my women, but she will be able to carry a lot of men and cargo, she will not necessarily be so fast, but she will be able to weather a storm well and that's what we need for where I propose to take her. I want to retrace our steps Olaf from several years back. I plan to go back to our palisade, to winter over and resume our exploration in the following spring. To further explore the coastline and land that lays to the south of the palisade, to take a year or even two accomplishing this task if need be. We can do any necessary repairs to the ship during the winter months much as we did before on our first winter behind the palisade before commencing our exploration of the coast. This time when we leave we will cache some excess stores and supplies there. If necessary we can return via our stockade and pick these stores up for our return voyage, a sort of insurance if you like, I don't want a repeat performance from last time when we suffered through lack of supplies and fresh water, with our clothes all in tatters and us barely making it back to Iceland, aye lad I had my doubts about us making it back home from time to time. I want to go back to our palisade and see the coast once more where we left poor Cnut and that old war horse Borg. Maybe the buildings within the palisade will still be standing, or at least repairable, I suspect we will be safe from the Skraelings there; they didn't bother us that first winter, so perhaps it will be the same again. I want a few options this time around. I feel it will also give confidence to the men if we are able to show them that Norsemen had lived and survived on this coast before and that we are not just sailing and exploring into completely unknown territory. I don't want us wrecked upon a shore with nowhere for the survivors to try to go , nowhere to resupply themselves, and feeling there was no hope of survival if things do go badly and then just having to wander the forests in complete despair until the Skraelings eventually find and kill them, or they die of hunger or exposure to the elements the very first winter. If we leave our wintering place at first break of spring, it will be my intention to sail to the entrance to the straits we saw, the one strewn with small icebergs and afflicted with all that fog in the early mornings, then turn immediately eastward and thence to circumnavigate that massive island that lies to the left of the channel, and chart the land there. To come around the southern tip of this island and enter into the mouth of the large river that lies opposite the western coast of the island, a river mouth so wide at its entrance that your mind will struggle to come to terms with it, so vast I believe it to be. This river is the real objective Olaf, how far will it take us, where does it go, what is the nature of the land, will there be unlimited fur to be trapped, antler horn and the precious bone from walrus tusks for the taking. Will the primitives be willing to start to trade with us? if so perhaps from them we can find out the location of any precious stones or gold. Once we have discovered its secrets we will return home and perhaps be able to return and guide other people who are willing to take a chance and colonise this land. I know that river is there for sure, all the signs in that strait indicated 'its presence, when we have finished exploring the land along the river, we will return back through those same straits up to our winter camp, we will rest and re outfit the vessel there and then return directly to Norway, or if the necessity arises we can put into one of the Icelandic ports. I feel I must do this thing before I die Olaf my one last great adventure, my final dream, so Olaf what do you say? will you come with me, will you risk everything that you have worked so hard for, and join me on what most people will say is an expedition of lunacy, will you come with me once more and cross the great western ocean'

'Yes I replied, without hesitation I will accompany you, I will sail with you to beyond the maelstrom and to the very edge of the world, where the water cascades from the ocean's end into the void of the underworld taking our ship to who knows where, and ourselves spirited away to the afterlife and Odin's hall if that's the way of things to come. If these things come to pass, you will hear no complaint from me, but I think you knew that would be my answer long before you broached the question Arn. However this time I feel you should be completely honest with our crew, and tell them exactly where they are going and the risks involved they after all may forfeit their lives if things take an unexpected turn. We should sail directly from Norway to the southwest coast of the Greenland and once sure of our bearings, strike out directly for the coast where our palisade lies. Most of our present crew will accompany us I feel sure, but will you ask any of the crew from the first trip of ours that took us beyond the western skerries to accompany us Arn'

The reply was not quite what I expected from him, but it showed to me he had at least thought things through.

'No Olaf,' he said

'They were, and still are all good men, but they have decided to steer another course through life and I will not be responsible for disrupting it, if I was to ask Bjorn or Ranald or even Geirr and his brother, they would think they were still oath sworn to me and it was their duty to come back for this voyage, I will not ask them to give their new lives up, and if things don't go to plan maybe their lives also, they all have families now and I won't have it on my conscience that I was instrumental in making their children orphans, just so that I could crew my boat with men I know and trust and all just to satisfy my selfish desires to see what lies up that river, I will not do it Olaf I will not be that selfish, therefore we will leave them to get on with their new lives.

'You are no fool Olaf you know the risks and you are right in this matter as always, we will impress the dangers on the crew we take with us, some of our old crew will be angry with me when they find out where we have gone and that we have not asked them to accompany us, but it's for the best this way, and the less people who know about our new voyage the better. If the people there in Iceland hear of our intended voyage they will want to form an expedition of colonists, they will remember that we have been to this land before, and we will be asked to guide them to the new found land, and that will distract from our true mission of exploring the land and ocean in more depth this time around. If we have a successful voyage of exploration perhaps we can return to Iceland and advocate a further voyage and take some colonists with us, if we ever did return to those lands with colonists I would want it well planned and organised, I would not be happy to hear of another Greenland disaster, where no one ever heard from the people who had gone there again and then have the fate of the colonists in the new found land on my conscience also.'

Arn purchased his new boat the following week, the old vessel "Sea eagle" that had served us so well and never really let us down, he decided to leave anchored at the edge of the beach just inside the Fjord. Some village traders had said they needed a storage hut, but as they had heard Arn saying his old boat was too costly to repair, they had asked him for the boat, for use as a storage barge instead of them having to go to the expense of building a new warehouse, Arn I know still remained sentimental about the vessel so I think he gave her to them asking for nothing in return, at least she would still be useful for a good many years to come. We decided to outfit our new vessel at Bjorgvin, away from prying eyes, if we had made it known in Bjorgvin that we were going on a voyage to Iceland, it would not attract any attention, plus it was the most logical place to do it, as everything we needed to supply for such a long voyage was here in the port or the surrounding villages. It would also prevent the original crew from hearing of our intentions, and become suspicious and guessing that our plan was to go back across the western ocean, thus doing things this way would prevent any awkwardness with Bjorn or Ranald, or the others as they would most likely not understand Arn's reasons for not asking them to accompany us on this voyage. Bjorn and Ranald could be awkward bastards at the best of times. We knew would also need a few extra men, which we hoped to recruit from out of the town, both Arn and myself were extremely well known amongst most of the seafaring men who drifted in and out of this port.

A few days later Arn, myself and a dozen of our crew boarded a friends knaar for the journey up to Bjorgvin in order to collect our new vessel, it being somewhat crowded onboard with all our kit, but not as bad as it could have been, as this voyage the knaar's captain had little cargo for Bjorgvin so he was glad to have a dozen paying passengers onboard. The rest of the crew were to follow in another boat in a few days' time.

As we came down the channel into port we saw anchored mid channel our new vessel, a magnificent looking vessel, gentle swinging on her anchor, we all knew that it was Arn's new boat strait away, myself and the dozen crew members all rushing over to the starboard side of the boat to gain a better look, my memory going back to that time long ago when we came to this same port with Ranald onboard, with him having us all in stitches of laughter with his antics of rushing from one side of the vessel to the other, in case he felt he was missing seeing something. This trip it was us doing the same thing and which had the knaar's master shouting at us to have a care least we capsize his boat.

The second day that we were in Bjorgvin I went ashore with Gunnar, an experienced sea man and to my mind a good judge of men and their characters. Arn and myself had already let Gunnar know are true intentions, that our voyage to Iceland was really just a cover story and that our real destination, was that of going beyond the western skerries once more, he had volunteered immediately, as we knew he would, what man of the North would not want to come on such a voyage of adventure and discovery. It was our intention of doing the rounds of the taverns, not on a drinking spree, but to put the word around that we were looking for men for a voyage to Iceland, we could not let it be known until we were sure of the men what our true destination was going to be. We went up the street and turned in to a maze of alleyways, and then turned left into a dead end alleyway, the street of the eagle as it was locally known, as at the end of the alley was a tavern of considerable proportions, a fish and eagle sign hanging over its door way, our old ships emblem had been similar, an eagle grasping a fish in its talons. The tavern had a reputation as being as good a place as any to meet sea going men, as well as a good drinking place. Just as we got half the way down the alley it was pretty obvious to me and Gunnar that a good old fashion tavern brawl was in progress, despite the early hour. We paused a few feet from the entrance, as two men were in the process of throwing another man into the alleyway, a second man quickly tumbled out onto the wet and stinking muddy ground, the comments coming from one of the men in the doorway resounding down the alleyway, identifiable as being the tavern owner

'And don't come back until you are a bit more sober, and if you ever pull a seax on one of my customers again there's going to be more trouble '

The two men picked themselves up from the filth strewn ground, arising more than somewhat unsteadily onto their feet, as they turned to face Gunnar and myself, I recognised the pair of them immediately, it was my old ship mates Tor and Reidar. I called out a greeting to them both, adding

'Hello boy's I see the Danes haven't gutted and filleted you then, I hear you have been on the whale road all these last few years and been raiding down into Dane land and down into the land of the Franks sailing up their creeks and rivers to attack their villages and towns and that takes some nerve I've been there myself a while ago, I'm surprised the pair of you have survived for all this time '

Recognition showed in Tor's eyes as he replied.

'Those Danes couldn't fillet a wet herring, and as for those Franks, nothing but men in frocks, we showed them a thing or two Olaf, be sure of that lad'

After a brief conversation with the two, it was again obvious that they were without a berth, having already spent the money they had gained on a couple of recent raids. All of these raids over the years had turned out to be as we had originally expected them to be, nothing more than an excuse to pillage under the pretence of it being a blood vengeance raid against a Danish king who had offered insult to Jarl Bjarni Thorfinn. Thorfinn had wanted to recover his honour, and make a profit at the same time;

but the Jarl seemed to have made a career of it as he had raided time and time again over the years along the Danish coastline, a brave or perhaps verging on being a stupid thing to do in my opinion. It was typical of Tor and Reidar wanting to accompany this Jarl on these voyages. On their return they had as usual frittered their money away on ale and women. So I had said to the pair of them

'Come down to the harbour early tomorrow, look for a boat called "Curlew" I have a proposition for the two of you.'

With that we entered the tavern to speak to the owner, to ask him to put the word around that we were looking for good men for a voyage up to Iceland and maybe some other destinations also. We were about to leave after having had a quick mug of ale whilst conducting our conversation with the tavern's owner, when he suddenly said.

'Of course you know that old bastard Einard is back, that last trip he made to the Shetlands turned out well, so now he's back with money in his pocket and he's on a bender, he's in the stable round the back, dead drunk laying on a pallet, he's been that way for two days now, I will be glad to see the back of him, he stinks worse than the horse, even the horse is beginning to complain, it's that bad.'

We both knew Einard well; a better man could not be found on the entire coast, and a good man to have next to you in a shield wall. He liked to drink when he wasn't at sea, but it was never a problem when he was on the whale road. We left word for Einard to come down to the harbour when he was himself again, it would be a waste of time, in fact even downright foolish even contemplating trying to speak to him at the moment, for he would be sure to fight any man who roused him from that drunken stupor, and even stupefied with drink he was something else to reckon with.

'Well Gunnar so far so good,' I said.' We have found three good men for sure, another three from somewhere and our crewing problems are over at least.'

Suddenly from somewhere done the street a voice bellowed out my name sounding like a bull stag in rut, and as we looked around for its source we saw a large man with long black greying hair that cascaded down to his shoulders which was plastered to his head from the recent rain, he wore a beard that reached down to his chest also flecked with grey, so that he looked like an old badger. He wore a sheep skin coat which came down to his knees with the fleece side turn inwards and it was embroidered all along its edges with red and blue swirling images. Across his back in a scabbard there was a curved sword and tucked in his belt he had a curved dagger with bits of coloured glass embedded in its handle, the like of which I had never seen before. He was forcing his way pass a couple of people who were trying to cross the street, soundly cuffing one of them around the ear who didn't get out of his way quickly enough. By the look of things this was not a man to trifle with or to get in the way of when he was so clearly on a mission. "My name is Yaropolk " he cried out, I come from the land of the Rus and I have just heard you are looking for some good men for your new ship. It took but the briefest conversation with this man for us to invite him down to the boat on the following day and offer him a place amongst our crew. I had heard of these Rus and thought he would be a useful member of our crew as he had told us that he had a lot of experience working on the river boats which traded up and down the rivers from his home town of Kiev all the way down to the shores of the black sea. His knowledge of river work might come in handy I thought when we were exploring the rivers and creeks of the new found land.

Tor and Reidar came down to the boat early the next morning as I knew they would. They could be hard to control but once they had given their word to do something then they would be as dependable as the next man, probably more so when it came down to a fight. Einard made his appearance at midday, he had all his kit with him plus a large skin probably containing mead, I did not ask him to give it up because I knew that once we sailed he would be sober enough. He looked a lot better than I though perhaps he would, according to the tavern's landlord the amount of mead he had consumed would have killed a lesser man. Anyway he would have plenty of time to recover from his hangover as we carried only a few barrels of beer onboard ship, and when that was gone there would be no more ale or mead until our return. Apart from a few private supplies of mead that would not last long we might have to go months without a drink. A day later and Yaropolk made an appearance with all his belongings and once onboard and his gear stowed he was eager to show his knowledge of working on this kind of vessel, he was as strong as an ox and we knew he was going to be an asset to us and he seemed popular with the rest of the crew from the moment he set foot on our deck.

After a few more days we had completed storing the ship, having managed to find a couple more men mainly on Gunnar's recommendations we now had all the crew we needed and all were now onboard. With the ship now fully supplied and everything in order we finally sailed and left the harbour behind us bound once more for the tip of Greenland via Iceland. Arn had rejected my initial idea of sailing directly from Norway to Greenland, saying he wanted to resupply in Iceland and give the men at least a day or so to stretch their legs; it would undoubtedly be too long a voyage without a break he didn't want the men exhausted when we came up to the new found land. So it was his intention for us to lay over for only a day or so, to resupply the ship and resume our journey to the tip of southern Greenland and once sure of our bearings strike out towards the distant coast where we hoped our palisade was still standing. Arn had told the crew everything he thought was necessary to assure them that thou we were going into unknown waters, to explore vast rivers and search for the land that allegedly lay south west of Iceland by a good many leagues. He was anxious to let the crew know that both he and I had wintered over in a place that we continually referred to as the palisade. We made no secret of the fact that the land we sought to explore was inhabited by fierce warlike Skraelings, that we had indeed lost men in a skirmish, but afterwards they had left us alone all of the winter. We would find our palisade and repair it and then settle down to maybe a few boring uneventful months until spring showed herself and we were able to start our voyage of exploration with all the summer and autumn before us to accomplish the task. Then we would be returning directly to Iceland or if needs be to winter over again at the palisade. I was repeatedly asked to tell and retell the stories from our first visit to these lands, which Arn encouraged, after all he told me it was me who had said we must hold nothing back from this crew regarding this new found land and what they could expect once we arrived on the coast.

We made Iceland and docked without incident, it was a voyage that all of us had undertaken a dozen times or more. On our arrival Arn and one of our new men called Flosi promptly disappeared ashore as soon as we were secured to the quay, Flosi I had heard of but had never met before, thou Arn seemed to know him well from somewhere. Arn left me in charge and told me to make sure the men stayed onboard the ship and not to engage in careless gossip with the shore side gang. They returned a couple of hours later, with Arn muttering under his breath and with hardly a glance at the expectant faces turned his way he disappeared aft, presumably to look at his charts, or just get away from the rest of us until his usual good humour returned. It fell to Flosi to tell us what the problem was and the cause of Arn's ill humour, the problem apparently being there would now be a delay whilst the island merchants were able to locate all the supplies that Arn had requested. It was fresh meat, fish and ale that now seemed to be in short supply, everything else we had already taken onboard in Bjorgvin. Flosi continued by bringing me into the conversation by saying Olaf will tell you himself that the last ship's crew when they returned from across the great western suffered more than a bit through running out of essential supplies. Arn is adamant that he will not allow it to happen again, so we will have to wait. The good news is that Arn has decided to allow you all ashore, but be warned he will not be tolerant of anyone who gets involved in any brawls, and for that matter any of you who can't hold their drink and start to babble about our true destination will find themselves in serious trouble. Arn has told the authorities ashore that we were on a voyage of exploration but that we were only going to explore the skerries that lay to the west and to try and find a landing on the east coast of Greenland. Most of us spent our time in the water front taverns, dallying with the local whores and drinking ale and mead, the time passed quickly and without real incident and within a couple of days we were all told to return to the ship, the remaining stores had arrived and we were to set sail on the morrow for the southern tip of Greenland.

We left port under a clear sky, the wind was fresh and we were all in high spirits, a few were the worse for wear having under estimating the local rot gut mead but all were looking forward to the start of our great adventure and were glad to be on an oar bench once more.

Almost ten days later and we sighted the peaks of Greenland, the winds had not been particularly favourable to us but at least we now had a last chance to check our position before pushing onto the coast that Arn had discovered all those years ago and hopefully he would be able to find our creek again where we had built our palisade. Within the week we sighted land, our men looking at Arn with nothing short of awe, this land lay exactly where he had told them it would be and that it was only a week's sail away from Greenland. Later Arn sought my advice and confided in me his obvious worries, we were on the coast again, but would we be able to find the creek again. If we could not find the palisade it would not be a complete disaster, but if it still stood it would save us an immense amount of work, we were also hoping that as we had enjoyed a conflict free winter there behind the stockade all those years ago then hopefully things could be the same again and the Skraelings would leave us in peace, we would be returning at the right time of year, when the Skraelings themselves would have other things on their mind other than war. A peaceful winter was what we needed in this place where we could just settle down to await the coming of the spring.

'Arn you will need the luck of Loki himself to find that creek again,' I said one evening when we were sat huddled in the stern of the boat out of the weather. 'The coast there is heavily forested; there are numerous bays that all look the same.' Arn then produced his charts, I saw that not only had he drawn the coast line and outline of all the islands, he had also around the edges of his chart drawn features of the landscape, such as high cliffs and rocks and he had detailed anything else that was of note or unusual, he had produced a superb chart.

That first morning that we sighted the coast Arn said to me.

"Unfortunately, Olaf as yet I can't recognise any feature of the coastline that lies before us, I don't know whether to sail north or south.'

So we elected to sail northward along the coast for a day and a night, when Arn suddenly announced that our palisade must lay to the south the way we had just come, when he told the crew it was the first time I had seen doubt in some of the men's eyes. No one said anything, you don't question your captain on points of navigation, most of the men spent years at sea but left to their own devises could probably not have navigated themselves across their local village mill pond, so we just turned southward once again.

Two days later and we came up to the entrance of a large bay; within the bay we could see a large island. The same thoughts were now going through my head as was obviously going through Arn's, neither of us said anything, the men were not happy as it was so we didn't want to raise their hopes to find that this was not the bay where Skeggi and old Borg along with Cnut had met their end at the hands of the Skraelings. Arn casually announced that we were putting into the bay for a couple of days, it looked like we were about to have a bit of a storm he said, which was actually true plus he said we could do with some fresh meat and water. Arn knew the risk we were taking, but it was his intention to land on the southern side of the bay away from where we had almost lost our boat the first time we entered this bay. Hopefully this side would not be frequented by the Skraelings and by the time any lone hunter could report strangers were back in the bay we would be long gone. We sailed the five leagues towards the far end of the bay passing the island to our left, I wondered what Arn was about and then suddenly it dawned on me. We came up to a shelving beach; I recognised it immediately Arn knew it was here, he was out to prove a point. There was a cry of alarm from Erik who was standing in the prow of the boat acting as lookout for rocks or sand banks and sudden shallow shelving of the beach.

'By Thor's hairy arse the white Christ priests are here before us, look up there on that cliff, the sign of their devil religion'

We all looked up, and there high above us was the cross still standing after all these years, the cross that Haggard had so painstakingly fashion for his Christian oar mate's lonely grave. If Cnut was looking down from his resting place he would now know that his vigil for all these years had not been in vain. I felt sure it would please him to see that men of the north had returned to this lonely bay once more.

I glanced at Arn and thought to myself that perhaps we should now call him Arn the lucky. The men had now forgotten their previous doubts, if indeed there really were any in the first place. I went onto to tell the crew that this was the very beach that Skeggi and Borg had died upon. That the cross they could see before them now marked our ship mate Cnut's final resting place. All doubt disappeared from their faces and I went on to say to them to never again question Arn's navigation, who else could have returned across the western ocean and found this place with such ease. We wheeled about now and crossed to the other side of the bay and anchored our boat in the shallows and waded up the shale beach, our boat now was hopefully obscured from the vision of any Skraelings on the opposite side. We wasted no time in locating a stream and were able to refill our water casks, while other men caught salmon further up the stream, others looking for shellfish amongst the rocks. Flosi and Gunner went ashore and returned a few hours later, saying that they had seen no Skraelings but had managed to locate some game.

That same evening I had to repeat the story again of how old Borg had held his ground with nothing more than a battle axe on this very beach to try and save two of his comrades and who had fought against overwhelming numbers of primitives before he was deprived of life and went to Odin's hall to sit with all men of worth and tell outrageous stories for all of eternity. It was the kind of story that the men never tired of hearing The next afternoon we left the beach and put out to sea, not wanting to chance our luck by staying in that bay any longer than was absolutely necessary. Arn now told the men that he knew exactly where we were and the palisade if it still stood was just around the next headland and up a creek a short distance. We managed to find a good strong breeze and raised our sail and fair flew along the southern side of this large bay, putting out to sea and coming about around the top of the headland before turning south for a league or two, and there to the right of us we saw the mouth of our creek. We furled the sail and manned our oars' and rowed against the current a half mile or so and there on the left we saw the land that we had cleared those years ago, the trees having grown back but were not yet as high as the ones that we had left intact. To our right was our palisade from all those years ago. We turned our boat mid-stream and anchored her. Arn turned to me and told me to go ashore with a few men and check the palisade out. We waded ashore and made an inspection of the outer perimeter, all the logs we had used in its building seemed intact, but they were being smothered with undergrowth and all manner of climbing plants. The gate still seemed secured and I bade Flosi climb over the palisade and remove the bar from across the inside of the gate. Within minutes we heard Flosi calling out that all seemed well, but it would be a while before he could clear the undergrowth from behind the gate to allow it to open. Several of us now managed to climb over and give Flosi a hand and presently we had the gates open and were hacking our way towards the two huts that stood in the centre of the stockade, all were intact but overgrown, the longhouse seemed to have fared the best. We entered the

165

large, long house that had housed the bulk of our crew all those years ago, it was intact and the crude table and sleeping benches we had manufactured seemed still serviceable, a few barrels were still stacked against the far wall, it was as if it was only yesterday I thought that I had last stood in this room.

It looked like some creature, a badger or racoon had burrowed under some of the logs and had made the place his home for a while in the corner of the building. There were a few dead birds, dead a long time ago by the look of them, probably having found their way into the building but never found an exit again. Grass and dead leaves had blown in under the door, cobwebs adorned the beams of the ceiling, but the place was still as sound as we had left it, possible seven or eight years previously.

I sent word back to the ship that all was well, presently Arn and the rest of the crew turned up to inspect their new home for the coming winter months, leaving only a few men onboard the ship to guard her and placing another two on the beach to keep an eye out for trouble. One of the men already seeing the watch towers ladder was still intact and had gingerly climbed up onto the platform to spy the land out. We commenced to clear the undergrowth from inside the stockade and put the huts back in order again. Arn and I along with Flosi and Gunnar being the senior men claimed the smaller of the huts as our own; the other hut could fulfil its original function of storeroom and cook house. As it was we had to split the supplies between the two huts and the longhouse, as we had brought a great quantity of things with us. We had numerous barrels of salted herring and salted pork there were also numerous barrels containing arrow heads, and barrel after barrels of arrow shafts, thou we would have to rely on finding local birds, or more to the point, their feathers so that we could fletch these shafts.. There were excess tools and weapons and coils of rope along with a large amount of lumber that we intended to leave here when we struck out on our great adventure. I knew what was in the back of Arn's mind. We were in this land totally alone, if things went wrong he wanted the men to know that there was somewhere to come back to, a place of comparative safety where we could organise ourselves and if needs be, if we really found that there was no way back home, we could live our lives out here.

The autumn passed into winter and the snow came early and confined us to our huts, we made repairs to the palisade and the huts within, and the creek began to ice over leaving us with no choice but to pull the boat up onto the beach. We did not want her frozen solid into the river and have her timbers spring, and worse still when the melt came the following spring we knew from past experience that the river would turn into a raging unforgiving torrent and would most likely break the boat out of her moorings for sure and see her drifting downstream onto the shore.

Now there was no escape if the Skraelings found us, but we thought it would be unlikely that they would find us this late into the season, even if they knew that we were here they would probably not do anything about us until the coming of the spring. They would in all probability think twice before attacking the palisade, especially if they had been watching us for some weeks before they mounted any attack and thereby knew that there were over fifty armed warriors living behind the walls of the palisade. Arn reasoned that thou we knew these lands were inhabited by Skraelings, it was most likely that in the immediate vicinity there would only be a few dozen families living together in one village. The land here and its resources, thou plentiful and on first face it would appear that there was everything they needed to guarantee their survival, it was likely during the winter months that it would still pose problems for them as resources would not be so plentiful in the full throes of a harsh winter and as such the land would not support hundreds of their people living in close proximity with each other. Which would in all probability even cause conflict amongst themselves

The winter came on quickly, with early morning frosts and bitter cold days, then one morning a slight dusting of snow covered the multi colour forest carpet of yellow and red leaves, only for a few days later for us to awake and see several feet of snow, the brows of the trees sagging under the weight of it all.

At the first sign of the thaw when the trees and bushed started sprouting fresh buds and the geese flew northward overhead once more and the creek turned not unexpectedly into a raging torrent for several days, sweeping all in its path downstream towards the open ocean. Then a few days later when the creek settled down to its normal flow and all large chunks of ice seemed to have disappeared from its surface we launched our boat back into the water, anchoring her out midstream. We checked it over for any damage, checked the ropes, renewing the rigging where necessary. Then the sail that we had stored in the large, long hut was brought out and taken onboard the ship. Over the next couple of weeks we stored the vessel and put the stores that were to remain behind in the palisade in order. After securing the palisade and walking the short distance to the edge of the creek most of us turned for one last look at what had been our home for the last winter, with most like myself wondering if we would ever see it again. We boarded our ship, manned the oars and rowed down the creek and out into the open sea.

Chapter Thirteen

This was the second time that Arn and I had left the safety of our palisade to once more continue our great adventure, having once again secured our palisade against man and beast. I briefly turned and took a final last glance at what had been my home for two winters, but it was quickly lost to view as we rowed the short distance down the creek and out into the open sea. The men were now straining at the oars with a will, glad that the winters idleness was over and that we were at long last back to doing what we had come here to do.

We followed the coastline southward as much as we could, only venturing further out to sea to clear the occasional peninsular or a rocky outcrop. After we had sailed what was most likely only a hundred leagues or more we sighted over the prow of our long ship what appeared at first glance to be the entrance to a large channel, as we continued further south we could see in the distance and to our left a large island, probably only some fifteen miles distance, it was shrouded partially in a low hanging mist. We altered course to take us closer in towards the island so that we could better see the nature of this land, eventually we began to lose sight of the mainland altogether. The men became excited and were asking Arn to put in so that they could explore what they thought were the shores of the new found land, the land that we had voyaged all this way find and to see if we could circumnavigate 'its entirety and to explore it's mysteries in-depth, thou I think that they were perhaps more interested in finding a creek to refresh our water barrels and perhaps to take a deer or a seal or two, we had lived well all winter and were finding it hard to go back to living on meagre ship rations once more.

Arn said with much confidence that he knew this land and that he had seen this island before, as indeed we both had on our first exploration of this area. This was the same island that we knew heralded the entrance into the foggy ice strewn channel that lay in front of us some miles further south, the channel that we had first seen all those years age. The bay that we had so aptly named the bay of wolves we knew lay over towards the right of us, on the mainland towards the west, but due to being shrouded in mist it was not visible to us. This was the bay where Guilli and Orn and myself had gone ashore and killed a deer, our time spent ashore had unsettled Guilli as he thought that we had been observed there. This had been the last day that we had spent on this coastline before our departure back to Iceland.

Arn assured the men this island was not the land that we sought it was not the new found land, but that we were close to what we sought, very close indeed. The men were full of confidence now, which grew in strength as time went by they now realised that Arn truly knew where he was going and that he had indeed seen these lands before, and that this was no haphazard exploration of a totally unknown stretch of ocean. Two hours or so later as we left the southern tip of the island away to our left we could now see looming up out of the mist a huge land mass, and as the sun rose in the sky and the mist dissipated a sparsely forested land showed herself to us on the horizon. As we closed in to this remarkable long-awaited sight we saw two headlands, which if we maintained our present course would have us entering a huge bay perhaps ten miles across and could well extend for several miles into the interior of the island. Arn decided that there was no gain in taking his ship into a vast unknown bay just to look for water and game, so we turned to our left and came eastward across the top of what we now took to be the coast of the fabled new found land we had so long looked for. We took the boat further towards the shore making the decision to anchor the boat in shallow water a few hundred feet from a piece of land that jutted out into the ocean. To the north of our anchorage we could see a small, forested island seaward from us perhaps two or three miles away. We sent a handful of men ashore to explore both up and down the beach for a mile or so and tasked another two with venturing inland for a short distance, to spy out the land here and see what it had to offer. Those of us remaining on the ship were barely able to retrain ourselves from dropping over the side of the boat and wading ashore to follow our comrades. The sight of this island and the smell of land and forest was tantalising beyond all belief after being at sea for so long. After what seemed an eternity the shore party returned and gave their report to Arn, with all of us crowding around them such was our eagerness to hear what they had seen. They described the land they had passed through, mentioning that they had seen no sign of man, or of his passing for that matter with no evidence of any hunters makeshift huts or the like. No remains of camps fires upon the beach, where people may had come ashore just for the night, nothing further inland was seen either. It was a good land with pine trees growing sparsely hither and thither with lush green meadows seemingly devoid of life, except for flocks of birds, but it would be somewhat strange if there was not deer and the like in the forests and meadows and there would be fish in the streams and rivers for sure.

After a brief consultation with myself and Gunnar, Arn decided that it would be worth the risk of us leaving the boat anchored where she was and leave a couple of men onboard to guard her, while the rest of us waded ashore and set up camp. It was his intention of staying in this area for a while as we still needed to replenish our water barrels and to hunt for game and fish the creeks it would be too good an opportunity to miss, as all seemed calm and peaceful here. After having had a winter of idleness, it was hard to get used to living on the boat again, our strength seemed sapped and our muscles ached from rowing and sleeping on the wooded decks.

Arn said he expected this island to be vast and if we truly wanted to circumnavigate it before coming about and entering the mouth of the river that lay at the bottom of the ice strewn channel, it could well prove an arduous voyage. However if the land on the rest of this island proved to be as hospitable as it was here then we should have no problems when we came ashore to hunt , and there will be plenty of time to rest. He continued unabated that he expected the voyage could well take many weeks or even months to complete. But he thought we could complete the task with time to spare and still be able to enter into the mouth of the river he so desperately wanted to explore. His thoughts were that we could voyage back to the palisade taking the short cut through the ice strewn channel with the winds in our favour maybe we could be back to the palisade in a few weeks hard sail, to winter over yet again. Then we could return to Norway, our ships hold full of furs and walrus tusk. Maybe others from Norway and Iceland could perhaps be persuaded to risk crossing the great western ocean and contemplate settling the land here once they had been told of what we had seen here, indeed amongst the poorer people back home they would want no persuasion at all, they would jump at any chance to improve their lives and escape the misery back home that most were forced to live in.

So we waded ashore to make camp triumphant in knowing that we were the first men to set foot upon this land and claim it for our own. It fell to me and Gunnar to go inland and see if we could bring a deer down, or at least to ascertain if the land hereabouts supported wildlife, another two men went further up the shoreline in search of a stream or creek.

Gunnar and I walked in companionable silence for a mile or so, he was a man of few words, quite the opposite to his younger brother Knut who was also onboard our vessel, Knut liked to joke and talk about all the other lands he had seen, the women he had bedded and all the drunken brawls he and his brother had got themselves involved in. Gunnar, ever the serious one of the two, often used to say that apart from the adventure and the possibly of taking furs and even finding gold, that he and his brother had no family back in Norway, no money for that matter so they had desperately hoped that the land we found here would be habitable and in the fullness of time be settled by people from our country, he was already well pleased I could tell with what he had already seen of the countryside around the palisade, and now on seeing this lush countryside had him further convinced of its potential and I didn't even need to ask him his thoughts on the matter as we continued our search for a deer.

It was not long before we were on the track of what we sought. We heard what sounded like a deer in rut, or as Gunnar put it sounded more like a reindeer from the northern part of our country. We had entered into some heavily forested land now and I for one hoping that we were going to find this deer fairly quickly, I didn't like the idea of just the two of us being out in the forest and straying into the path of half a dozen Skraelings out hunting themselves. Gunnar bade me stop and stay silent, he had seen some movement in the undergrowth just to our right, a further rustling sound and then a huge bellow from the animal, the wind was blowing from the animal towards ourselves, the animal was as yet unaware of our presence and he came further into our line of sight, a huge beast that looked similar to one of our moose back home, but much bigger, I certainly had not encountered one this large before, it was a magnificent specimen with a huge spread of antler, but as the pair of us knocked an arrow each to our bows, I still felt some remorse for what we were about to do, but we needed meat for ourselves and the rest of our crew, so we loosed our arrows. Our arrows flew true but as soon as the beast felt the barbs he thundered of back into the forest with us close on his heels, but suddenly he stopped and turned with what I thought was a bewildered look upon his face, if animals can ever be described that way, and then he crumpled onto his front legs, he tried briefly to regain his feet and then rolled over onto his side and stayed that way, he was already dead when we came up to him. As Gunnar began to butcher the animal he bid me go back to the beach and gather a few more men to help carry the meat back to the ship, there was an immense amount of meat here and we needed it all, as we had well over fifty men to feed, and he obviously did not want to have to abandon any of our kill to the local wolves and foxes. I was about to argue and say I didn't think it wise to leave him on his own here in this forest, but thought better of it, I could return with help in well under the hour, so all should be well.

I returned with a few men to find Gunnar had more or less finished his task of butchering the beast we had killed, he had nothing to report other that he sensed there were a wolf or two lurking in the distant trees, attracted by the smell of blood no doubt, but not willing to investigate further while Gunnar was still present. Our men, feeling the same as myself about being out in the forest wasted no time in wrapping the meat into manageable loads and slinging it across their shoulders we started back for our boat, making good time back along the forest paths and towards the beach and our ship. Within minutes of us departing we heard the snapping and snarling of wolves, fighting over the scraps of gut and bones we had left behind us on the forest floor. We arrived back onto the beach with aching shoulders to be greeted with a couple of fires already lit, the men wanting to waste no time in preparing our meal, one that would be well appreciated after having endured a few weeks of having no fresh meat.

We left our bay a few days later and preceded south ward, hugging the coast and taking in the land, anxious not to miss anything of interest or something that could provide us with more information about this land of plenty. We sailed for many miles presently passing two islands to our left presently coming up to what looked like the entrance to a large bay or sound, but we knew we could not explore every bay and river we came upon so we contented ourselves with anchoring close in and with the bulk of us taking the opportunity to sleep ashore and cook our evening meal upon a roaring fire at the edge of the pebble strewn beach. We felt secure, after having left our last anchorage without again seeing any evidence of human occupation, however we still posted look outs and thought if there are any problems with Skraelings we could deal with any situation that came our way, thou if we actually encountered any Skraelings Arn I knew would prefer that we just board our boat and sail off rather than get involved in any more pointless skirmishes with them.

Our sense of security and well-being turned out to be ill founded because the very next morning we were awoken by shouts from Einard and Sturla, who were running back to our make shift encampment. They had wandered up the coast a ways to check on something that they had heard during the night and went to investigate the source of it, perhaps as much to elevate the boredom of their early morning watch. They said that they had thought they had heard voices and went to have a look in that direction, only to find half a dozen Skraelings asleep beneath two small up turned boats, how ourselves and these Skraelings had managed to camp so close to each other and not be aware of each other's presence was a mystery. Their boats were small and Sturla thought that they were covered in seal or walrus skin. They had awakened immediately when they had heard Einard and Sturla's footsteps on the pebble beach; they then apparently came from under their boats already holding their stone axes and another two were quickly laying arrows across their bows.

'It happened so quickly there was nothing else we could have done Arn, other than defend ourselves, there were six of them they would have killed us for sure before we could have come back here to raise the alarm '

Einard then continued by saying

'The ones armed with clubs attacked us, so we defended ourselves and killed three of them, the others taking flight leaving their boats behind on the beach'

Arn looked at the two of them with that withering glance of his and both Sturla and Einard squirmed under his gaze and were left in no doubt that Arn thought they had mishandled the situation. They had incurred Arn's wrath that's for sure, they thought what they were doing was the right thing, believing that there was no other course of action open to them but to fight these men, I must admit had I been with them I think that I would have done nothing differently to what they had elected to do, but I could understand Arn's stance on things, he wanted no more violent contact with the Skraelings.

Sturla was getting a bit angry now and repeated Einard's words

'What else were we meant to have done? They would have followed us back here and attacked the rest of you as you slept'

We could see that Arn would not be pacified by words alone ; he still fair seethed and raised his voice which was uncharacteristic of him.

'First the two of you wander away from our camp, leaving the rest of us sleeping and un protected and then

179

you start to murder some of the very people that we are trying to avoid conflict with, and whose help perhaps we may well be glad of one day. We left three of our own good men dead back there behind us on the mainland, how many more of us would you have these Skraelings kill? '

'We are here to explore, possible even to try and trade with these people in the future, and see if this land can be colonised by our people. Now we have set these people against us, these men were most likely just out fishing or hunting, now they will go back to their people and let them know they have encountered strangers on their shores, they will come back in numbers and seek us out for sure, they will be looking for revenge. Let us go now go back to where you last saw these boats and look at them and the remains of their camp site to see what manner of people we can now expect to encounter'

Sturla and Einard stood there shaking their heads, but when Arn led a group of us back up the beach they sheepishly followed, but the boats had gone and they had not left anything behind other than their dead, even the dead men's weapons had been taken. We looked at these men all clad in animal skins. They had long hair and bore blue tattoos upon their skin and looked to be well fed and healthy. We left them as we found them, suspecting that perhaps their people would return for their bodies later when they knew we had gone, Arn said he didn't want to antagonise the Skraelings further by interfering with their dead. We left a couple of seax and a few arrows wrapped in a deer skin with the bodies, perhaps they would understand from this it had been a mistake, but in the end they still had lost three men to our violence and a few trade goods would not make up for that. We all looked around nervously, half expecting that we were being watched as we stood grouped around the bodies lying prone upon the beach. We gathered our belongings from the beach and returned to our ship, all of us now anxious to be away from this place before the Skraelings returned in force.

Now and then for several days afterwards as we continued southward along the coast we saw people on shore, others started running along the beach trying to keep apace of us. It was unlikely that these people had heard of our conflict as yet with others of their tribe, they were probably just curious or maybe they were alarmed and wanted to see what these intruders into their land were doing. Now and then we saw two or three people in small boats similar to what Sturla and Einard had seen back along the coast. Some tried to follow us but could not keep pace with us. Arn said had things been different perhaps we could have stopped and tried to speak with them, but as things stood he thought we should be away from this part of the coast as soon as we could. We would undoubtedly encounter more Skraelings farther down the coast and if conditions seemed favourable then we could perhaps have another attempt at speaking with these people.

We had favourable winds and sailed ever southwards but after a few days Arn sought my council and confided in me that before winter set in we would have to just follow

181

the coast and see where it took us, he said he was of the opinion that if we continued our present course this close into land we would sooner or later inadvertently enter a channel that will lead us into a dead end, therefore I think perhaps we should now turn to the east and stand out to sea a bit further, we can put into land to hunt and to search for fresh water, even to explore if we see anything of interest. I don't want to waste time exploring deep channels and bays, only to have to return the same way we came. I don't want to winter on this island if I can help it, I really want us to come about the southern side of this island and enter the river mouth that I now know lies at the bottom of that ice strewn channel we have already ventured into. I feel that on this island we will be in continual conflict with the Skraelings, they seem more numerous on this island than back on the mainland where we wintered in comparative peace.

In the following days' time after time when we put into shore, to hunt and to explore, we saw evidence of occupation by Skraelings, and more times than we would have liked we now saw smoke on the horizon, remains of camp fires on the beaches and several times saw men in small boats entering or coming out of creeks and into the ocean. On occasion we came unexpectedly upon Skraelings, they either took flight on seeing us or behaved in a threatening manner, waving their weapons at us and occasionally firing their primitive arrows at us. All attempts on our behalf to communicate with them was to no avail, and we already knew that to try and set up a permanent settlement in these lands would be to hazardous as we would always be in danger from these people. They seemed fierce to the extreme and it was obvious that they would not tolerate strangers on their shores.

We sailed for days passed rugged countryside, not so dissimilar to parts of our own lands, the climate was mild for this time of year we thought, we were now entering mid-summer and we all sensed an urgency on the part of Arn to complete this circumnavigation of this island as soon as was possible, which left us less and less time to hunt ashore, on the occasions that we did go ashore we hunted not just for food but also the fur bearing animals that inhabited this land. A few men searched in the mud and silt of the river and creek beds for evidence of gold, but we found nothing. We sailed now southeast ward, standing out to sea a distance of what we considered to be twenty or thirty miles, clearing headlands and rocks, until on the third day after about the best part of a hundred leagues or so we realised we had lost sight of the coast. Arn saying now that it was most likely time to turn southward again, he felt sure he told us that we had now travelled all that there was of the northern coast of this immense island, one evening he showed me his chart of the area that he was presently working on. Slowly he was adding to this chart the outline of this island, the ice strew channel and the land that we had wintered in already lay drawn there in front of us on his vellum chart. He was a fair chart maker in my opinion and entered even the smallest detail. We turned into towards the west again

183

presently picking up the coast line once again. Our plan had been to put into a bay that we could see in the far distance and resupply ourselves with fresh water, also to give some of us the opportunity to hunt for deer, to go fishing and perhaps hopefully take a few more furs, but as we came closer onto the coast we realised the bay we were about to enter was tidal. We stationed ourselves of the coast well out to sea and we could see the rise and fall of tide within this bay was immense and the general census of opinion was it was not worth the risk to enter this bay and maybe risk losing the ship. So we stood out to sea again and once we had travelled as far south as we could following the coast line we turned due east for about a hundred leagues, presently coming up to a group of islands. We had no choice now but to put into land, our water barrels were getting low and we had been used to eating well, so now it was essential we find a good anchorage. Once ashore we set ourselves to fishing and we found that the streams and creeks were full of salmon and easy to catch. We found that were not the only fisherman on the streams and inlets; in the distance we could see several brown bears catching salmon as they made their way up stream jumping the small waterfalls to reach their spawning grounds. The water was pure and we soon had our water barrels replenished. Gunnar and I went off with our bows, taking Flosi with us to keep an eye out for Skraelings and leave the two of us to be able to concentrate on our hunt, we managed to bring a large deer down after a couple of hours or so. We gutted the deer where we were and risked a small fire where Flosi cooked some of the offal, which was a welcome addition to our diet, but as Gunnar pointed out we had hardly been suffering the last few months, we were probably having to easier a time of things and getting soft.

'Speak for your-self Gunnar chided Flosi, I for one could get used to this kind of easy living'

We returned to our boat anchored of the beach to find that Einard and another man had also had success with their hunt. Some of the other men had stayed and tried their luck fishing in the nearby creek and caught more salmon than we could possibly be able to eat, so they had started to smoke the excess meat for leaner days.. When all of us had returned to the ship the main topic of conversation was whether anyone had seen any sign of Skraelings. We dallied amongst these islands for the best part of a week with no sign or evidence of Skraelings, until one evening Arn announced that in the morning we would resume our journey. We had cleaned our water barrels and they were all now full of water. We had dried fish and meat and a couple of the men went hunting one last time before our departure and came back successful.

We sailed for about thirty leagues in a north-westward direction after we had lost sight of the coast line of the new found land. Arn announced that he thought we had crossed the bottom of the ice strew channel that we had once entered into from the north. Directly to the north off us lay the bay of wolves he casually told the men, I knew he was telling them this because it was essential for him to appear as if he really knew these waters that we were navigating through, it was not arrogance he knew it was of the utmost importance for the men to have faith in his abilities, if their confidence was lost they could well force Arn to turn the ship about and head for home saying that he was putting their lives at risk for no gain. We were totally in Arn's hands, his confidence showed and the crew never doubted him or faltered once. He said we were now about to enter the mouth of the river that continued ever west ward. He knew it there, this is what we had come to this land for, to explore its banks and go as far as we could up its reaches. We still had most of the summer still before us, this is where we would find the abundance of furs and horn and perhaps some gold, this is the prize at the end of it all. To the north we had already taken a large amount of walrus ivory so we thought that there must be more riches along the banks of this mighty river that we were about to enter. We sailed on presently seeing a large low-lying island starting to reveal itself, we elected to keep to the southern side; it looked more like a huge sand bar than island, with only sparse vegetation covering it. As we sailed past it we gauged it to extend almost a hundred and fifty miles by our estimation; we kept to its southern shores with Arn saying this was further evidence of the immense river that must now surely lie ahead of us and the power it must possess to be able to create such a large sandbank

Chapter Fourteen

We now knew that we had entered the mouth of the river that we had sought for so long, thou we did not realised it for a day or so, our first sign of us being in a river was when someone drew water and noticed it no longer tasted salty it had become brackish. Arn was ecstatic at the news he had always been so sure this river existed, it's been here since time immemorial he often told me, travelled only by a few Skraelings in their primitive boats most likely unable to comprehend its vastness and importance.

'It's been patiently waiting for our return for us to explore its furthest reaches; we would have discovered it earlier had I been more daring on our first voyage. I had told myself then that we were short on time and it would not be prudent to come through that iceberg strewn, foggy channel I hesitated perhaps through fear, but there's a time for caution and there's a time to grab what you want with both hands Olaf, remember that when you have your own boat and have to make your own decisions, there's but a fine line between recklessness and calculated gamble'

We sailed when we could, but mainly we had to row hard against the strong current. It was on about the twelfth day that we had left the safety of the river bank early long before the dawn had broken, the sky towards the west was bright red, we had spent the night anchored a hundred feet or so off a shelving shale beach, it's true to say the men's moral was still good and that they were still in high spirits. Arn I knew was pleased with the men's performance over the last few months, having hardly heard any complaints from them at all, and things truly seemed to be going well perhaps too well he had once said to me.

It had the promise of a good day and we all sensed that we had arrived at the turning point of our long voyage, this was what we had come all this distance for, this is where Arn would make this country give up all its treasures and wealth and show us the full extent of its riches and all of its secrets would be laid bare, this land surly had much to offer.

We came to a large river mouth to our right which Arn proposed to enter and to explore its reaches for a day or two just see if it entered into a bay or find out where it led, we would discover it's secrets and then return down the same way and re-enter the large river which we were presently navigating and continue westward. We made our turn and rowed with a will up this new river there was dense forested land to either side sometimes coming down to the river's edge in other places it was much sparser and the forest gave way to large rock-strewn beaches. As morning progressed the sun rose and burnt of what remained of the river fog from the previous night. Later towards noon the sun showed herself high in the sky we found ourselves in brilliant sunshine, towards the north there was the remains of a rainbow but it was still quite cold still despite the us having the sun upon our backs, we thought that we were now about to enter early autumn. The trees we could see along the bank had turned their leaves a golden orange and red, some had fallen already to the ground and were slowly forming a multi coloured patchwork of colour beneath the trees. Despite the chill in the air it still made for an exhilarating pleasant day. As we progressed up the river we could now hear in the far distance, the sound of roaring water, as if it was perhaps cascading over a water fall or such, but it seemed so far up ahead of us that most of us were not concerned. Arn was concerned thou, he was always looking to what lay ahead and trying to participate any unforeseen problems, it was what most likely had kept him alive all these years. I could see his brow creasing as he stood with me in the prow of the ship as we both strained our eyes to look into the distance up the river.

'We must pull over to the river bank shortly and beach the boat if at all possible, perhaps it will be a good idea to make an early camp, I am thinking that come the morning we need to send a scouting party up ahead, and find the source of this water fall or rapids, its making me un-easy lad, I don't want to proceed much further until I know what lies ahead of us'

A little later, as we rounded a slight bend in the river, we were still well in mid-stream of the river, when suddenly we lost the warmth of the sun with a fog seemingly been sent by Loki himself to frustrate us and make us feel even more apprehensive then we already

189

were, it embraced us and caressed us in its damp and numbing coldness which seemed to get into the marrow of our very bones, drops of water were forming on our clothes and made our hair and beards glisten. The fog was so dense that we literally could not see our hand in front of our faces; two men had already been stationed in the prow of the vessel, one with his lead line calling out soundings and the other lookout standing as high as he could in the prow shouting back to the rest of us the obvious; that he could see nothing. Alarmingly thou we could now hear what most definitely were rapids up ahead, but it was a different sound they assured us from the other roaring cascading sound of water which we had been hearing for some hours now.

Almost immediately after that, another cry came from the lookout stationed in the prow, a warning much too late

' Broken water, rapids ahead.'

Both men now started shouting at the top of their lungs, but we all knew we had left it far too late to pull over to the shore, in retrospect we should have acted sooner on Arn's instinct, hind sight is a wonderful thing. Things I sensed where about to go very wrong for us, my premonition proved correct because within seconds we found ourselves being hurtled and bumped across what at first seemed quite shallow rapids, we would have appeared to have gone from deep water into rapids in a few thousand paces, how could the river shelve so quickly ? We had been going up river against the current, the wind being in our favour but now even the direction of the current seemed to have changed it was now completely confused like two seas meeting out in mid ocean, we had been so sure that we would find a lake or a bay not rapids and most likely further up river we thought there must be a waterfall that fed this anticipated lake and thus the river itself. That at least had been our first thoughts when we had heard cascading water. I could see the look on Arn's face and felt his anguish asking himself how he could have made such an elementary error of judgement and been so stupid in wanting to bring the boat so far up a small unknown river in this land whose mysteries we were still trying to unravel.

We could hear the hull of the boat scraping across the rocks beneath us. The thick rolling fog bank prevented us from seeing what lay ahead of us and thus what the best plan of action should be, Arn did all he could and ordered the helmsman to put the boat over to the right hand side of the bank, which hitherto had seemed to have the deepest water there, but it was impossible we had no control over the vessel it was like another hand was now at the steering oar, with one intent alone and that to send us to our doom, then quite suddenly we were spirited over to the left hand side of the river bank and were swept into deep water and what seemed to be a whirlpool, with a high cliff face above us, but the accursed fog even denied us any glimpse of our impending fate. The entire boat spun round as if it was a child's spinning top, and just as suddenly we were spat out of the maelstrom like a man would spit an apple pip from his mouth, we now hurtled through a narrow gorge, into what appeared to be a secondary channel of the river, the vessel was buffeted by rocks either side of us as we went, then like a miracle, as if Thor had waved his hand and countermanded Loki's will and commanded the fog be lifted and it disappeared as quickly as it had descended upon us. We were being pummelled by rocks from either side and beneath us, so narrow was the channel we had been pushed into. We were being forced towards a rock strewn beach to the right of this narrow gorge, which slowly opened up in a much wider channel, deceivingly giving us hope that we were away from the worst of it, but even as the steersman called for the oars to be manned, Loki perhaps annoyed with Thor's intervention played yet another of his tricks upon and as the boat slewed 'sidewards the rocks on the river bed ripped through the timbers of the keel of our boat, like a fisherwomen sliding her knife down the under belly of a herring while filleting it , but even so there was still enough force in our momentum to cast us up upon the beach. We came to a sickening lurching stop, men were thrown out of the boat into the raging torrent, some being cast upon the rocky beach and others falling heavily within the boat itself. After the initial shock of what had happened we started to come out of the daze that we had all been thrown into. We began to pick ourselves up from the bottom of the boat, those thrown from the boat onto the beach were beginning to stir and were now checking themselves for broken bones, with all of us looking around us to see where Arn was, or to try and see a comrade that they had been sharing an oar bench with only minutes earlier. Mainly they looked for Arn, their captain the man who always knew exactly what to do. We gathered on the beach and began to get organised as best we could, we stationed a lookout down the beach to watch for Skraelings, we thought it unnecessary to keep much of a lookout to the left, the way we had come in through the gorge, no one in his right mind would contemplate coming through that hell hole in a small boat. I called all the men to attention on the beach to check to see how many of the crew were missing, I thought I had seen Einard flung from the boat, what a way for the poor old bastard to go, a fine oars mate and warrior lost to Odin in a stupid wreck. I hoped I had been wrong but Sturla confirmed it and said he had seen him thrown from the boat, adding almost matter of factually that Hrapp was also missing.

Our charismatic Rus Yaropolk lay face down in the shallow water which now gently lapped the beach, blood seeping from a head wound his blood mingling with the current and flowing downstream from whence we came, for him to have come all the way from his beloved river Dnieper which he spoke about so often, only to die like this on a small river of no consequence made no sense at all to me. Twenty others at least were un accounted for and we could only assume they had drowned, another two men lay dead in the bottom of the boat. One with his head at un natural angle, the other one, by the look of things been thrown against a splintered plank which had gone straight through his chest.

We hoped that perhaps this beach we now found ourselves wrecked on was remote enough from the prying eyes of any Skraelings who were out and about, something always on our minds as we knew full well that this land was inhabited by people more than capable of waging war on us, as our experiences from a few months back had shown us. The Skraelings thou were but a secondary consideration at the moment, we chanced a fire to dry our clothes and to cook some food, while the remaining men and myself walked back to the ship, one only had to look at the boat to see it was hopeless to even contemplate any repair, you didn't need to be a boat builder or carpenter to figure it out, the keel in front of us lay broken in several places, you would not think that the power of water could snap a boats back with the same ease that your wife snapped twigs to feed a reluctant fire first thing in the morning.

She had been a sturdy vessel and now in a short space of time it was nothing more than potential driftwood waiting to rot on the river bank. Arn had been thrown from the boat, but had made it to the beach unharmed. Now as we sat on some rocks together to discuss what the best plan of action was, Arn being ever open to suggestions as to what we all thought was the best plan of action. We had absolutely no idea of the lie of the land here, never having ventured far from the river banks. We thought that to try to repair our wrecked boat was out of the question as also was trying to build another boat. We had lost most of our tools and equipment, we also had the potential problem of not knowing how long we would be able to stay here unmolested by the Skraelings, certainly not long enough to complete the task of repairing the ship or even building another one of sorts, even if it had been thought feasible, what then? Would the boat have then been sturdy enough for us to sail it back down this river, through that fog and ice berg strewn channel and out into the open sea, I for one doubted we could build such a boat and where would we go? Not straight back to Iceland, it was impossible even to contemplate undertaking such a voyage, we would have to try to return back to the stockade, but the God's would be against us making it in a repaired or makeshift boat. Arn shook his head like a shaggy dog as he turned and spoke to me

'Olaf we will have to walk out of here and go back to our stockade on the coast on foot carrying just the absolute essentials. We left a great many supplies there, weapons and tools and even the means to make another sail for a boat is there, timber as well, enough to make a small boat, which is of course, assuming the Skraelings have not ransacked the place, and Olaf I fear we will only need a small boat, we are going to lose men on this march. We will have to recover our strength over the next few days and leave before the winter sets in maybe we will have to winter over somewhere else, it's going to be bad Olaf but I can think of no other course of action, if we can get back to the stockade we can stay there for as long as we need, knowing that we are most likely safe there and that we can live of the land indefinitely, We left those supplies there for just such an emergency as this, we are not finished quite yet we can survive this situation.

But Olaf the problem is the distances involved it's a terrifying march that faces us across unknown territory before we could reach safety of the stockade, I estimate it at almost two hundred leagues to the north east of us'

The pair of us felt in slightly better spirits now at least we had formulated a plan, so when the men had recovered a little from the initial shock of the situation that they now found themselves thrown into and came to realise they were not for the after world quite yet, we would put our plan towards them such as it was. At least we would now be able to give some reasonable well thought out answer to all their questions, thou in all likelihood they would not like what they heard.

Our thoughts were suddenly interrupted by shouting from further up the beach, intermingled with other voices, it almost stopped my heart from beating when I realised I had heard that language before and knew what men were now amongst us, I also knew that we were as good as dead because of it. I could see Tor, who was closest to Arn and myself pointing down the beach, he had seen our lookout was in trouble, in fact the man was now down on the sand, even from this distance we could see the two arrows protruding from his back. The bulk of the Skraelings must have been in the tree line and now they targeted us with their bows, bringing several men down. Tor and Reidar, closely followed by Sturla had recovered their wits quickly, and all three being armed with shield and axe charged up in to the tree line, and were amongst the Skraelings archers before they had even realised that they were in danger. The Skraelings seemed not to want to get involved in hand-to-hand fighting with our three men, and quickly tried to disappear back into the forest, but not before our three men had extracted a terrible retribution upon them, leaving six or seven of their number dead or dying upon the ground by my reckoning. Arn shouted to Reidar to bring his men back to the beach and not to pursue the Skraelings further into the forest.

We slowly recovered our wits and when we had calmed down sufficiently we begin to appreciate that we were now in a real predicament. We began to bury the bulk of our dead men in a common grave with their weapons, most were Christians and we thought it an appropriate way for them to be buried where they fell. The man, who had been killed down on the beach whilst acting as lookout, had been called Bran and came from Iceland and was one of Odin's believers and had been with Arn for quite some time. More sadly thou, he was a good ship wright as I remember, the God's surely had abandoned us, to lose men was bad enough but to lose a man skilled in boat repair and building was hard to come to grips with. We built a funeral pyre at the edge of the river and sent him on his way to sit with his brothers and await the call to arms and the end of mankind.

All seemed quiet for the rest of the day and throughout the evening, we half expected to hear the natives chanting and banging their drums in the forest prior to a dawn attack, as we had all those years ago when we first had encountered fought this race of people. All was quiet until the afternoon of the following day, the quietness of it all having almost lulled us into a false sense of security.

Suddenly the Skraelings launched their second attack, they charged out of the forest and down onto the beach yelling and whooping like banshee's what must have been their war cry, trying to frighten and intimidate us, but had they known the men that we were, and where we hailed from and were to understand the character and the resolve associated with men off the northlands they would have realised that they were wasting their time. We were not cowardly Friesians or Danes, we were men from the far Northlands and we had all been born for such a day as this. Loki had brought us here to this accursed beach to fight these primitives, to prove ourselves as men. Today was the day that had been waiting for each of us all of our lives, soon we would enter Odin's hall and take our place at his table, but first we had to prove ourselves to Odin that we were worthy of that place, we must all die like a man of the north should with sword or axe in hand with our foe laying slain at our feet, we must fight our last battle without complaint, no thought of surrender until we are eventually overcome and succumb to our injuries and then and only then will our spirit leave our bodies and be spirited back home and to Valhalla.

They must have known that they had hurt us badly on the first attack. Apart from myself and Arn, the only other able body men left in a position to mount a defence were

Sturla and that incorrigible pair Tor and Reidar, we formed a five man shield wall, with the wreck of our vessel behind us, forming a protective area for our wounded men, men that were now unable to participated any further in this last fight, Gunnar and his brother sat propped up with their backs against our wrecked boat, both leaking blood from numerous wounds, Gunnar had a severe head injury, with half his face caved in, both had their swords in their hands ready for one final blow against the enemy if they could manage it, but they both must already have realised that they were not too far away from answering Odin's call, ready to embark on their final journey to the afterlife and to an eternity of feasting and drinking at the one eyed bastards table in that great hall that we all so longed for, to be able tell all and sundry off our exploits and conquests in life until the time came for us to participate in that last battle the world would ever know, before the world could be reborn again.

Eric and Jorge were laying there either dead, or perhaps unconscious to wake no more in this life, perhaps already having already taken their seats next to kin and friends at Odin's table and were eagerly awaiting the coming of the rest of their comrades. Flosi had taken an arrow in the throat and two more in the chest; he was still breathing, but would be on his final voyage shortly. The Skraelings had attacked with great force; time after time they threw themselves against our small shield wall concentrating on the centre where Tor and Reidar had positioned themselves. I saw Sturla on the far end of the shield wall go down completely overwhelmed, Arn next to him, trying to support him, staggering himself under a fuselage of blows, most he seemed able to ward off with his shield, but it was only a matter of time now. A blow suddenly came from under my shield, jolting me back to my senses and my own precarious predicament, a stone headed axe striking me on the shin, which sent me sprawling, these savages were learning quickly how best to fight us. Tor and Reidar seeing the three of us in trouble moved forward trying to draw the attention of the Skraelings away from us, all thoughts of maintaining the shield wall now gone, there had not been enough men to form it properly in the first place, but these two warriors were giving Arn and myself an opportunity to regain our feet, but it was far too late for Sturla by the look of things, he would not rise to his feet again, at least not in this life. Tor and Reidar fought like berserkers from the stories of old and I could see the Skraelings stall, their line checked, not quite sure what to make of these two warriors, their ferociousness putting doubt and maybe even respect into the minds of kindred spirits. I was back on my feet by this time, thanks to Tor and Reidar's actions, but I was being hard pressed by two huge Skraelings, both with stone axes, my lime wood shield had splintered and was not much use to me now, I took several blows to the body, my leg I knew was not going to support me much longer, and then a blow to my neck followed by one to the side of my forehead saw me tumbling to the ground, another blow and that's all I knew for quite some time, until I regained my senses once more, wondering where I was and if I was still in the land of the living or whether I had passed over to the other side. The light was failing there was a slight drizzle, I looked around me and surmised I was still alive, thou the God's only knew why I had been spared, I guessed I had been unconscious for a good few hours.

I looked around, my head was aching and I could feel a lump as large as a hen's egg on my left temple, the skin seemingly having split, and it was obvious the wound had leaked quite a lot of blood, but which had now congealed upon my face and neck, my leg was extremely painful and looked how it felt, really bad. As my mind cleared I wondered what had happened, why had I been left alive by the Skraelings, I looked behind me, Erik and Jorge were still in the same place as I had last seen them, these two brothers were still propped up with their backs against the boat, both still had their swords in their hands. Next to them sat Gunnar he still had his arm around his young brother's shoulders, I didn't need to go over to them to know that they had all passed over to the other side, probably at this very moment entering Odin's hall. The pair of them had at last found the land and peace they searched for, Loki had played his final trick on these two brothers or perhaps he had only given them what they had sought for all these years, but now it had been replaced by certain eternity in Valhalla.

I got to my feet and looked around, Sturla's body was still laying at the edge of where we had initially formed our shield wall, the bodies of Tor and Reidar were laying some distance away where they too had fallen in battle, looking at them it seemed to me by the way they were laying on the ground, that they had fought back to back, until finally overcome by sheer force of numbers. The Skraelings seemed to have removed their dead, and dead there would have been as we had given a good account of ourselves but at much too high a price to bear. I looked for Arn's body, but could not find it expecting the worse, because I could not see how he could possibly have survived this attack.

I began to search the tree line for him thinking that I could at least give him a proper burial, I came across him shortly, it looked like he had managed to crawl away from the beach and now sat with his back propped against a huge tree, his sword in his hand, his discarded shield at his feet, he appeared to be dozing but as I hobbled over towards him he opened his eyes and called out a greeting, but in that moment I could see that he was mortally wounded, a Skraelings arrow shaft protruded from his chest, midway up on his right hand side, he must have tried to pull it out, but the arrow had snapped asunder leaving what I guessed to be the best part of two inches or so of shaft in his side, the stone arrow head now wedged in his rib cage but had gone in much deeper originally, he tried to speak again but just a gurgling sound came out, he started coughing, bright red blood that frothed and bubbled, and ran down his chin, he wiped it away and tried to smile, I knew he had suffered a death wound as I suspect did Arn himself, but still he was trying to give that infectious smile of his which I had seen so often.

I could not fathom out what had really happened towards the end, Arn was in no condition to put his opinion forward, I can only surmise that the Skraelings had thought they had killed us all, but it was strange that none of our weapons, clothes or anything else for that matter had been touched or taken away, or perhaps stranger still that they had not mutilated the bodies of my fallen comrades, that was the way of some tribes of people back in the north lands and in the land of the Rus, so why not here with these people also. I kept returning in my thoughts to the look on the Skraelings faces as they faced Tor and Reidar in their final battle dance, was it respect from them towards these two brave men that made them leave the bodies on the battle ground unmolested, or was it just that we were no longer of any importance to them, being just another vanquished enemy whose bodies they would leave to rot and for the crows to pick the bones clean.

With the failing light came a dramatic fall in temperature, it began to feel decidedly cold, the drizzle and dampness in the air making things much worse and it began to sap my will, I knew that Arn and myself would not survive for long in these conditions, so I immediately set to building a shelter of sorts. A few yards away from where Arn sat I saw that a pine tree had fallen some time ago, broken off a quarter way up its trunk, falling so that it had snagged on another tree as it did so. I thought it would make a basis for a shelter so I began to cut some other branches from an adjacent fallen tree and propped them up against this fallen trunk either side, and over this I threw part of our sail over the frame work of branches, thus forming a makeshift tent or at least something that could be called a shelter and at the front I draped another part of the now ruined sail from our boat. I dragged Arn into his new home and made him as comfortable as possible, placing a cloak across his body that I found discarded by the remains of our ship, I think it was Knut's who had discarded it prior to the attack, he wouldn't need it himself now that's for sure. I found myself completely exhausted after all this effort, and thought that if the savages had heard me as I made the shelter, and came to investigate, it would be just too bad as I knew there would be nothing I could do to mount a defence of any kind, in my present state of mind it was not worth the effort to dwell more about what could or would not happen. With that in my mind I closed my eyes and quickly fell into a deep slumber.

The rain falls heavily now, I think that winter has come to this land early this year, I can hear the wind howling through the trees above the beach, its threatening to rip the roof from our make shift shelter, I am now too weak to stand let alone to go outside to do anything about it, my leg is extremely painful especially when I try to move, it has tuned black from the foot to well above the knee, I know it's not broken, but just badly cut, swollen and bruised. We must have been in our makeshift shelter for several days now, I glance across at Arn, he appears to be asleep and has been that way for many hours and is making a strange rasping sound as he breathes, I have decided not to wake him, I have no food or water left to give him anyway, what little we did have I have consumed, and Arn is in no state whatsoever to take anything, he is long past that, besides I don't think I could reach the river for more water and return again to our shelter. I think that he will never wake again of his own accord. I have placed his sword so that it lies beside him, within easy reach of his right hand. When he's finally gone to meet his ancestors and all his friends, to sit with them in the hall of Valhalla, I will leave this place and seek my own destiny and try to walk back to our stockade, but for now I to will try to sleep.

When I awoke I was confused and disorientated, not being exactly sure where I was. I had slept fitfully tossing and turning upon the hard ground, the pain from my leg preventing proper slumber, my dreams had been full of screaming Skraelings running towards me I wanted to run, to hide to be as far away as possible from these demons, but men of the north do not run away from a fight. I never before had such thoughts or dreams never in my worst nightmares so why is my resolve faltering now, why has my courage deserted me. In one of my dreams Arn was standing on an open plain the wind was ruffling his hair and the fox fur trim of his cloak, the sky was dark and overcast above him, the grass rippling in the wind and appeared to be purple, he was beckoning me to come forward and then as I advanced the entire land became filled with Skraelings, feathers stuck into their black hair and all brandishing war clubs with shields upon their arms, their faces were painted with bands of red and black and they filled the distant land as far as the eye could see, as far as the snow-capped mountains on the distant horizon. Then all of a sudden there was a flutter of wings and the Skraelings had all turned into ravens and flew high into the sky and the sky became so black it blotted out what little sunlight there was and the noise from their beating wings was so loud it hurt my ears. A raven landed on my shoulder and started to whisper into my ear, then I awoke with a start, it was already late morning and I was soaked in sweat, my head ached and my leg was agony, but I was still alive but I was thinking strangely now, maybe the blow I took to my head had rattled my brains, I was thinking that perhaps it would have been for the best if I had slipped away in my sleep, after a while however I did find that I was in many ways feeling a great deal better and I guessed that I must have slept for many hours, it was early morning the rain had ceased at last and the wind greatly diminished. I glanced across at Arn, he must have woken briefly during the night, as I can see his sword is now grasped firmly in his hand, he looks at peace now and I know without even crawling over to him that he must have died a few hours earlier, so typical of him not to wake me, not wanting to disturb my sleep in his final moments, never wanting to inconvenience anybody, or was it because this time he knew he was about to embark on his final voyage, and like all his voyages in life there had been no one to guide him, so now as always he would want to start this voyage alone, the greatest adventure of them all. My friend, a great man and adventurer gone, it was almost unbearable, Arn had been a true man of the North, a warrior when need be, but mainly an explorer and trader of note, always searching for habitable hitherto un-known lands, especially if it meant he could guide poor people to these lands as potential colonists, people who were not as lucky as himself, perhaps reformed criminals, slaves or outcasts, people that had not had the opportunity to improve their lives because of lack of money or did not have the freedom from oppression to prosper back in their own homelands. Many would have been willing however to follow him to these new found lands if given half the chance, hoping to improve their lot, it mattered not to Arn, everyone was entitled to a second chance in his book, but I cannot say I feel that sad now, I have seen all my comrades die over the last few weeks, most were sent on their way on funeral pyres or on makeshift barges down the river, a few who were Christians are buried in the surrounding land around what remains of our ship, but sadly most of all I have had to leave seven good oar mates unburied besides our boat, the site of their final battle. I will return later and do for them what I can. When the time comes for me to answer the final call and go to Odin's hall, if I were to be asked if it had all been worthwhile I would have to say in all honesty it had indeed been worth all the broken bones and the cold and damp, the poor food that made our teeth fall out. It was the adventure and of things to come that continually drove us forward, we were born free men in the northlands it was the path Odin had decreed that we follow and I for one had no complaints.

After a while it seemed to me that I had recovered my strength somewhat by the next day, and I managed to pull Arn's body out of the make shift shelter and with effort I scooped a hole in the earth and buried his body and put his sword back into his hand. I then placed rocks and boulders on top of the grave to stop wild animals from digging the body up again. I hoped that Arn would understand and forgive me for not giving him the Viking funeral he deserved but I knew that I had neither the strength to carry his body down to the river let alone to be able to make a raft or such to act as his funeral barge. I fashioned a wooden cross and placed it above the cairn, I'm not sure what made me do it other than I felt the grave should be marked in some manner, I really don't know if Arn was a Christian or not, he often spoke to the contrary saying he followed the old ways, but I vaguely remembered him spending quite some time all those years ago back in our village, at old Hans house where Hans and his Christian wife, Hilda I think her name was, were nursing back to health an injured Christian Scotsman that they had rescued from the sea and who preached the white Christ's teachings to all who would listen to him, I know that after theses visits Arn was more tolerant towards the Christians he came into contact with than he hitherto had been, unusual for a man of the north, it was also rumoured that the Scotsman had some connection with Ranald who I had sailed with for several years and who had been with us on our first voyage to these lands. The lad we had taken from that beach in Scotland all those years ago and who had come to live amongst us and who had become a true man of the north, and it seemed to me that Arn had made no secret of the fact that he had a soft spot for the boy. I didn't get to know Ranald to well, despite sharing an oar bench with him for a quite a while but he did do well by us and was a good man to have next to you in a fight.

I returned to the shelter and stayed the night, determined to go back down to the beach and bury my friends the next morning before leaving this place and go to who knows where. Overnight rain water had accumulated on the sail cloth covering our shelter and I was able to quench my thirst without the struggle of going down to the river, my leg was still causing me great pain, it having turned overnight into various colours of purple and yellow, as I washed it with a damp rag I noticed there was no offensive odour coming from it, and it did seem to me that the swelling was beginning to diminish, this I took as a good sign and I hoped it was therefore on the mend. I fashioned a crutch out of an ash sapling which aided me greatly in getting around and I wandered back to the remains of our ship, hoping to find food, supplies and weapons to equip myself for my forth coming journey to seek out my own destiny in this land.

On my arrival at the beach the boat down on the beach was still as I had last seen it after the fight with the Skraelings, the bodies of my friends still laying there. The rain by now had once more turned to snow and there was a heavy dusting of powdery snow now covering their bodies. I searched and found my bow in the bottom of our wrecked boat, my rowing bench, which also had doubled as my sea chest had split open from the impact of the wreck, but I managed to retrieve some spare arrows, the seax my father had giving me when I left home that first time to join the 'Starling', which now seemed a very long time ago. I spent some time collecting various other useful bits and pieces of equipment and clothing. In the bottom of the wreck I found some dried fish and seal meat, which had not yet spoiled so for once in many days I was able to eat as much as I wanted, washed down with some mead that I found in a skin. The rest of the day I spent dragging the bodies of my fallen comrades to the edge of the tree line, I placed them side by side and covered them with their cloaks and pieces of the sail from the ship, putting their weapons next to them and then proceeded to cover their bodies with stones from the beach, it took an awful long time to complete the task due to the fact that my leg was causing me problems and pained me greatly, I had to go further and further afield to find suitable large stones and slabs for the job. I wanted to be absolutely sure that their bodies were not going to be disturbed by wild animals. Once done I had a last look around the wreck site for anything else that may be of use to me on my journey, but where I thought I was going to travel to still remained a bit of a mystery even to me at this moment. I could only think that perhaps I should try to return to our palisade, it would at least give me purpose and an adjective to aim for. The snow began to fall more heavily now and I returned to my shelter for the night determined to make a start first thing the next day.

Chapter Fifteen

The dawn broke and I awoke with a start, I was sweating profusely and my whole body was shivering. I looked outside my shelter and found that there was several more inches of snow which had fallen during the night and now lay on the ground completely covering the undergrowth, with the tree branches sagging under the weight of it, the sky was grey and laden with snow, the wind which had probably awoken me was whipping the snow up into flurries, it seemed very cold, the snow was dry and if it snowed again, as indeed it looked as if it might well do, there would be several feet of it very soon. My mind went back to my first trip where we had wintered behind the stockade that we laboured so hard to build, but that place was at least two or three hundred leagues away to the northeast, the winter there had been harsh, and I had no reason to suppose that it would be any different here, but at least there we had been prepared for it and had ample supplies. This time thou I was painfully aware of the fact I was on my own, with no supplies and shivering and cowering under a totally inadequate shelter, I would not survive it I grimly thought. I had to change my plans, I could not go off into the forest to explore this land without any purpose or destination in mind, not with the onset of winter, I could not wander aimlessly around until I succumbed to the cold or wild animals or maybe worse. Come spring if I survived maybe I could resume my journey living of the land and make it back to the palisade, but first I would have to survive this winter, I would have to stay here and build a log cabin from the timbers of our wrecked boat and also utilise the pine trees growing in abundance here. I would have to take the chance that the natives would leave me alone and not come back to this area at least until the spring. With the winter over I could start my journey and see if I could travel back to our palisade, at least there would be clothes and weapons stashed there, shelter too if nothing else. But I also feared the place might well be full of my fallen comrades ghosts, searching for a way to Odin's hall, so many were not given a proper Viking burial and would now be denied entrance to his hall having had no time or opportunity to grasp a sword to their dying hand before they passed over to the other side. They most likely would now be condemned to an eternity of walking the shores of the great eastern lake, perhaps now and then looking upwards in response to a seagull squawking high above them, the spirit of one of their brothers also being denied Valhalla, having drowned at sea and now like them forced to wander the world until it was time for it to be reborn again, for better or for worse. Perhaps some solace could be gained knowing that they would not be totally alone.

But first things first, I would have to go out into the surrounding forest and see if I could bring down a deer. If

I was to have to work hard, which I knew I must if I was to succeed in my attempt to quickly build a cabin and get ready for winter I would need some good food and plenty of it.

I think at this moment in time I was at my lowest ebb, in reality if I had been truly honest with myself I knew the chances of me making it though the winter were at best slim, even with a cabin of sorts for shelter I would be relying on finding game in the forests to hunt, but last time that I wintered over I remembered that when the weather had closed in, and sometimes it had for days on end it had prevented us from stirring from the palisade by more than a few feet from its perimeter. I knew it to be a delusion on my part but that's what man does, man is born with the instinct to survive from cradle to grave and without this instinct we would not carry on, and we would achieve nothing and would falter at the first real obstacle.

So I left my make shift shelter, taking a good look around me at the country side, doing my best to get my bearings so that I would be able to find my way back again. With one more backward glance at my shelter I turned and entered the forest proper. As I meandered through the forest, trying to keep my bearings and not get lost I could see through the trees above me that the snow was falling heavily, the tree branches beginning to sag under its weight. The forest floor was clear still in a lot of places, but that would soon change and makes the forest paths un passable. I had not seen any large game, nor any evidence of there being anything here, I had been in the forest for several hours, I had killed a couple of what looked like hares, but the deer I sought eluded me. Suddenly I wandered into a clearing, and there in front of me was an old man and boy of about ten years old, they had brought a deer down, a huge, magnificent stag and now I presumed were struggling to get it back to their camp, wherever that was. I could imagine their reluctance to butcher the animal there and then, and just take what they could easily carry, knowing that when they returned for the rest of the carcass it would be gone, taken my wolf or bear, either way it would be taken for sure and they would also lose the valuable pelt. I cursed myself for being so careless and wandering so clumsily into these people, the very people that I had wanted to avoid at all costs. The old man seemed as startled as myself and was probably feeling just as foolish as I was for devoting his attention wholly to his kill and not to what was around him. The boy recovered first and notched an arrow to his bow, I instinctively pulled my shield from around from where I had it slung across my back looping my arm through its straps I held it in front of me tucked into my body, my right hand instinctively going for the axe in my belt. As soon as I did this I saw some flicker of recognition in the old man's eyes, he said something to the boy and laid his hand upon the boy's bow, shaking his head. It was obvious that the old man knew who, or rather what I was, a survivor from the battle he must have heard about. I advanced, without really thinking about the consequences of what I was doing, I was certainly taking a big risk here, but perhaps these people could be my salvation, I needed to show them I meant them no harm, so I indicated to them that I was willing to help them with their deer, a few seconds passed before the old man understood what I was about. I cut an ash pole from the edge of the clearing and tying the deer's feet together slid the pole between its legs, two of us would now be able to shoulder the deer and carry it away, I hoped their camp was nearby, because the deer was heavy and was going to be difficult for the three of us to handle. My leg pained me greatly and I was surprised I was managing as well as I was. We camped in the forest overnight, I managed to get a fire going and we cooked the two hares that I had killed earlier in the day. The old man had saved the deer's liver and kidneys and other bits of offal, which we toasted on sticks over the fire, they seemed willing enough to share anything they had with me, which was precious little. We spend a cold and restless night sleeping best we could around the fire, none of us were really well equipped for spending a night out in the open.

The next morning after a few hours walk we came up to their camp at what I judged to be about midday the following morning, our shoulders well and truly aching now from the weight of the deer, to make my misery worse I was by now limping badly.

I don't know what I had quite expected their village to be like, but it turned out to be just a small village of perhaps six dwelling places in a forest clearing, and another two at the perimeter of the village and by the look of them in need of some repair, the place seem poor beyond belief. The smell of the place was appalling, which I later came to realise was normal in all these Indian villages, there were dozens of dogs running free and barking at me, knowing I was a stranger in their camp. The entire village had turned out to inspect me, whether I was guest or prisoner now lay in the old man's hands. My presence with the old man and the boy would seem to have been reported by the camp lookout some time before our actual arrival. The village seemed to be comprised mainly of old men, women and children. There were only two or three other men apart from the village lookouts who were of a warrior's age, but I seemed to sense straight away that this was no warrior's encampment, rather just a few families struggling to exist side by side in this harsh environment. I was ushered into what would appear to be the old man's home, a very aged and decrepit looking woman was tending a fire in the centre of the hut, the smoke spiralling upwards eventually finding its way out of a hole in the roof, a clay pot hung over it, from which a not unappetising smell emanated from. Many furs were on the floor of the dwelling, a spear and shield adorned one wall, with a bow and quiver of arrows hung on a peg near the entrance. The only good thing about the place was that it was warm inside. The old man left me, and I guessed that he had gone to join the other men to discuss what should be done with me. The old women looked at me with curiosity, but showed no fear of me, giving me dried meat to eat and some water in a container that seemed to be fashioned from some kind of gourd. That night I slept in the old man's hut undisturbed, and the next morning I was taken to the outskirts of the village to where a dilapidated hut in need of much repair was shown to me. It was evident that they were offering me somewhere to stay, one of the men then pointed to my bow and then at the hut and waved his arm in a circular motion and then pointed back at the hut, so from this I understood that they were saying I could stay and hunt and live here with them, for a while at least.

As I came to know these peaceful and generous people, and as I picked up a few words of their language it transpired that their numbers had been greatly depleted a few years back, originally they had been a much larger and prosperous tribe but now mainly through starvation and injuries sustained in defence of their village against other natives they had lost a great many people, they seemed not to mention illness; all of them now looked remarkably healthy, considering how they lived. A neighbouring tribe had been particularly hard on them for a number of years. Many of the men folk had been killed, and a few women and children abducted. Which is why they had made the decision to relocate to this remote area to rebuild their village, an area away from the river and one which the other tribe did not often frequent, it was poor land not suited well to cultivation and the hunting was sparse. They thought that here they would at least be left in peace, and besides which they now had nothing left to offer this other tribe, by now they having taken everything. It would have been this other tribe that had attacked my people the old man of the village insisted. This was probably the reason that they had some sympathy and empathy towards me, thinking this tribe had done to my people what it had also done to theirs, they knowing that they had killed my friends and supposing that they also had also stolen everything we had, but which was not quite true in our case, the river having done that before we encountered and were forced into a fight with this hostile tribe.

I busied myself over the next few days repairing my hut and then in the weeks that followed spent most days out and about hunting, sometimes the old man's grandson accompanied me, slowly I found the lie of the land, so that I had no problem finding my way around to the best parts of the forest for hunting and most importantly being able to find my way back into camp. I always took more game than I needed for my own use, if I shot a deer I would skin it and keep a small portion for my own needs and give the rest to the old man and his wife, who I knew then distributed it to the other members of the tribe who were in need, especially if they had not been able to hunt that day or had not been so successful as me. They showed no resentment towards me and their friendship towards a stranger in their village was quite surprising. The pelts from the deer and hares that I had killed I cured and then tried to turn into clothing in the same fashion as the natives wore. My own clothes were in tatters and I felt the cold, especially in my injured leg, although it had now healed I knew it would never be quite the same again. The injury had left me with a slight limp, more noticeable in the cold of the mornings. I tried as much as I knew how in trying to sew some of my pelts together to form a cloak but alas it was evident my skills did not lay in that direction, and my endeavours were a source of amusement to the other villagers, in the end I think it was most likely the old man who told his woman to sew some clothes for me. So one day he sent his granddaughter to my hut to collect my furs and pelts, saying that they would make me something better than what I was presently wearing, which should not be too difficult they thought, their sense of humour always shone through and along with their uncomplaining view on life helped them endear themselves to me. The granddaughter was a shapely girl, verging on being plump as it seemed all the women of the tribe where, when they were well fed. She was a happy girl, with a permanent smile and always had a good word for everyone; she had raven black hair so different to the women I had known back home. When one day I made her a present of a necklace made of bear's claws, you would think I had given her the world, such a simple undemanding and uncomplicated people. I was taken with this girl strait away, and she for some reason with me. One day I returned from hunting, I could smell and see wood smoke coming from my hut, the smell of cooking meat tantalising my stomach as I had not eaten throughout the day. I dropped the deer that I had shot in the forest outside the entrance to my home and pulled aside the deer skin covering the door not quite sure of what to expect only to find this women tending the fire, several bundles of furs and other domestic things I recognised as belonging to her were leant against the wall of the hut. She offered me a bowl of food and asked if I had been successful in my hunt after that there were no more questions, it seemed that I had acquired a wife, a situation that was perhaps connived by granddaughter and grandmother, perhaps because I was so slow in saying anything, and in this harsh land time was not always a luxury one could afford, but it was an arrangement I was extremely happy with, as were all the other members of the tribe. In all the many following years that we were to live together I don't think there was ever a cross word spoken between us.

This woman who could not speak a word of my language helped me settle into the life of her village. In the early days before I fully learnt her language and truly settled down it had been at times a struggle for me to realise my former life was gone forever that my existing with these simple people was now my new life. I slowly came to terms with it all knowing I would never see my homeland again nor ever hear my native language spoken to me again. She helped me find a peace within me, a peace that I had not even realised at first was missing. Now I had found amongst these people a true contentment I had previously thought not possible. During the nights when sleep evaded me for some reason bringing with it the demons that live and thrive in the dark, bringing with them those un characteristic darker thoughts of my past. I often recalled what my father had said to me when he repeatedly had asked for me to join him on our boat, fishing out on our local Fjord and to put all these thoughts of travel and supposed adventure to one side, nothing good can come of it he often told me, you have a good life before here as I also have had and my father before me, consider staying and embrace the life you were born to. Now after all these years I know what he was trying to say to me, but of course at the time I would have none of it and went my own way.

In my even darker thoughts I questioned myself as to why I had acted and done the things that I had, tormenting myself with memories of all the terrible acts that I had committed, all the men that I had killed and yet worse maimed, most did not deserve it. To kill to protect one self and that of your oar mates and keep your boat safe and secure was one thing, it was to be expected of a man of the north or anyone that would call himself man, but when my mind turns to other thoughts, especially to all those people that I and others had killed when we raided up and down the English coast, which in reality was nothing other than pure thievery and murder of innocent people but it was easier than honest trade. Arn would never go raiding but as a last resort, he was a enlighten man for a Viking. I had learnt so much from that man and still missed his guiding hand. But what of all those monks in the Scottish monasteries that we attacked, all were defenceless but we had murdered them all the same and stole their relics. We told each other that they were evil men because they followed the ways of their nailed god which we had not even tried to understand, but it was evident that they were willing to die for their religion so perhaps we should have realised there was more in it than at first we thought, but they were not followers of Odin so it was of no matter that they died and we were happy to see them on their way to whatever they though lay before them in their afterlife. How many of us were really willing to die for Odin? I had often asked myself that question and never liked the reply. I remember cutting the throat of an aged priest as he knelt in front of his altar, a calm acceptance of his fate and the smile upon his face he realising that he was about to meet his god still haunts me to this day, but he stilled died under my knife and for no good reason that I can think of other than it was expected of me to kill him and all those like him.

These thoughts now haunt me less and less as I have now become content and realise that I have now become one of the richest men in the world here in this simple village, I now know that all that hack silver, gold and precious stones that I and others sought for most of our lives is not of any importance, I have my woman and child, we sleep in a warm hut during the cold winter nights and eat well. The village is disease free, there's game in the forest to be hunted and fish in the rivers and nearby ocean just there for the taking. I can walk through our village and find myself welcome at every hut, this is what is really of importance the rest is inconsequential.

Now and then when I go out hunting on my own, or with my small son I often make a detour and come to the very edge of the cliff high above the mighty waterway that I and my companions had entered all those years ago, even from high up on the cliff edge I can hear the water as it surges across the rocks and onto its destiny further up river to who knows where. I now realise that there are further lands, most likely un-explored even by the Skraelings further up along the river banks, with the untold wealth in furs and gold that we searched for in vain, it's there for sure. I know it's there just as Arn had always known it to be there and its riches are there in abundance, the further you travel westward all you will find is more and more un-explored land just waiting to be taken. The far west doesn't lead to the edge of the world as some people back home in the northlands would have us believe, there's no fetches or monsters in the rivers and sea's awaiting to devour your ship the land simply goes on for eternity, that's my belief.

Now as I look to the east down this mighty stretch of water towards the mouth of the river perhaps in my dreams hoping to see a long ship, its sail billowing out in the strong breeze, with men sitting at their row benches grasping their oars, their brightly painted shields hung out on the shield rack on the top strakes of the boat, I can image their straining, aching muscles as they row hard against this unrelenting current, now I think that I can even see the ship and hear their voices, and the chant of the helmsman as he tries to keep the row stroke constant, but suddenly I am jolted back to reality by my small son, tugging at my breeks and I realise that I am looking for a vessel that will never come, I know I must resign myself now to the fact that I am the last and only man of the north upon these shores, I make a mental note that I must take my son when he's older to visit Arn's grave and pay my respects to him and to all my other fallen comrades who's bodies will remain for eternity in that place, and also to show him what remains of our ship and what men of the north are capable of and help him understand his father's people and where we came from.